Shadows of
Mulberry

Shadows of Mulberry

by Gwendolyn Nebelsick Mahler

Disclaimer: This is a story of Lexington Kentucky Society, high powered business and the eventual demise of a family dynasty. It is written as I lived it or was as told to me. It must be mentioned that at times this author took journalistic privilege in changing the names to protect family privacy. I present to you—Shadows of Mulberry.

ISBN 978-1-58597-461-0
Library of Congress Control Number: 2008924659

LEATHERS
PUBLISHING
4500 College Boulevard
Overland Park, Kansas 66211
888-888-7696
www.leatherspublishing.com

Acknowledgement

I wish to acknowledge Athalie Mathews who wrote a class paper (circa 1958) regarding Dawson Springs, Kentucky and some of the people in Shadows of Mulberry which I have gleaned some descriptive information. I also wish to thank the Hart County Historical Society in Munfordville, Kentucky (especially Carolyn Short), the Horse Cave Heritage Festival Committee for the reassurance of my facts in the book A Leaf in Time and my new friend, Ann Matera, in Horse Cave, who all assisted me in finding this family.

I would also like to thank Ann Vernon, Editor and the women at Leathers Publishing, Barbara Thomson, Madlyn Davis and Michele Rook.

Especially, I would like to thank my sisters, Lulu Lee and Claudette in making these memories come back so clearly.

Dedication

To my late husband, Captain Fred who would have enjoyed seeing this book to completion.

*...For though from out
Our bourne of time and place
The flood may bear me far
I hope to see my pilot face to face
When I have crossed the bar.*

Alfred Tennyson

Table of Contents

Prologue

It was the wild, lawless thirties—turbulent times in Chicago. Idalynn Brooks was most unhappy with the diverse lifestyle in which she was living. Along with being extremely lonely, she was extremely fearful. Her husband, Michael, had tried to explain to Idalynn, that violence was the nature of his career and although she had agreed to accept life with Michael, it was now difficult for her to do so. She felt her marriage to Michael was a terrible mistake.

Idalynn found herself sinking into dark depths of despair with sorrow of choices she had made with her life. She yearned for her gracious lifestyle back home in Lexington, Kentucky, when her responsibilities had been few. She wished that she could go back to that time of her life. Idalynn thought to herself, had she only married Roger Edmonds, she would at least be home in Lexington. Idalynn, obsessed with returning to Mulberry, the family home in Lexington, knew what she had to do.

Urgent Journey

The Jumbo Jet soared majestically through the air. Suzanne Brooks was going home to Lexington, Kentucky. Although it had been many years since she had lived in Lexington, Suzanne still possessed tender memories of those earlier days. It was the hard to explain childhood memories of living in a family with continuous emotional struggles—remembering them still that caused tears to well in her eyes. There had been so many doubts, and so many insecurities to be resolved; yet, Suzanne knew it was unproductive to reach back in time, trying to solve any of them.

Suzanne gazed out of the window as the plane flew through the clouds, toward the Blue Grass Airport. The low ceiling, with the solid overcast, was perhaps appropriate for the day. The urgent telephone calls from her sisters, Lee and Emily this morning to her in Kansas City, where she was employed as an airline stewardess, informed her of the sudden and unexpected illness of their mother, Idalynn Brooks.

Idalynn Brooks still resided in their Lexington home on Versailles Parkway, three blocks east of Wilson Avenue. This was the home that Idalynn's father, Charles Spencer, had bought for her mother, Lulu Lee, many years ago and now, once again, Idalynn was privileged to be living there. Suzanne could not help but wonder what the future of this lovely home, Mulberry, encompassing all of the family's history, would be, if, something were to happen to her mother.

Turning from the window, Suzanne rested her head against the back of the seat and closed her eyes. The hours of flight seemed devastatingly long. The tides of sadness were descending, as the memories that had been safely locked away in her mind began to unravel.

With the sound of the plane's engines in the background, Suzanne reflected about her family's troubled past. The so-often-told sad stories of their lives weighed heavily upon her. She questioned to herself, *how anyone could have possibly withstood all that had transpired within this legendary family?* She had always been told that her ancestors had been survivors. She only hoped that her mother would be a survivor, now.

In The Beginning

Suzanne's great, great grandparents, John and Mary Spencer and their three sons, Daniel, Arthur and Robert arrived in America in 1865, through Ellis Island, having sailed from Isle of Ely, Cambridgeshire, England. Charles Spencer, Suzanne's grandfather would be the third generation of this English family.

While John chose to settle in the state of Kentucky, where his wife had laid plans to do her missionary work, his brother, Edward, who had also come along on the crossing decided to remain in the eastern section of the United States, thus accounting for many of the Spencer family socialites and physicians in New York and Palm Beach. Some of the second generation Spencers settled in Houston, Texas, as was evident with the Spencer Department Store that had at one time been in business there.

John and Mary chose to establish their home in the beautiful hills of Western Kentucky in a small, quiet village called Madisonville. It was there they raised their children to maturity. Their first grandson, Charles, would be born in 1879. It is with Charles that this story begins.

Sixteen years after settling in Madisonville, John and Mary Spencer chose to move to an area eighteen miles south that would later be called Dawson Springs. John Spencer and his friend, Irvin Hamby, founded the town, and drew up papers for incorporation. This area was named after a local man, Mr. Dawson who had donated the land, making it possible for the railroad to come to the area.

Dawson Springs was a quiet small town, nestled in the hills of the beautiful bluegrass state. The wooded hills and the valleys, along with the magnificent views of the Ohio River, created a compelling desire for so many to live there.

Shortly, after having arrived in this new area, John accidentally discovered mineral salts water, while digging a cistern. Being an astute businessman, John had the water analyzed. Analysis showed that the water had many minerals that were believed to have curative powers for people's health.

Prominent doctors endorsed the water, and people came from all over the country and abroad, proclaiming the water had granted them complete cures, whether the complaint was disease of the liver, kidney, bladder, rheumatism, gout, dropsy, or even female irregularities. It was not uncommon to see people arrive from the train on a stretcher, in a wheelchair or using a cane; and after a few days of mineral baths, return to their homes walking without assistance. It was possible the cure was a matter of "power of suggestion;" or perhaps, it was that same pleasant environment felt by the town's people that contributed to the person's convalescence.

With his children and grandchildren assisting in panning for the salts, John was able to start a family business of manufacturing and selling salts, which became very successful within a short period of time. And this was the beginning of the Spencer's dynasty.

———————

Charles Spencer, being the oldest of John Spencer's son, Arthur, was the first grandchild to be initiated into the family business. As a young lad, Charles worked side by side with his father and grandfather. Throughout his life, Charles had only fond memories of his stable and very happy childhood in Madisonville.

Traveling for his grandfather's business enabled Charles to become a very independent and self taught person in the business of sales. Although he was of small build, appearing to be younger looking than he was, he had earned the respect of all of his clients. As his two younger brothers, Albert and Frederick became older, they too, became salesmen for the family business.

I'm Mr Charlie

It was August, 1898. Charles was on a selling journey with his father's automobile, a Ford Quadricycle, to Horse Cave, Kentucky. Horse Cave was a small community located in the center in the Great Cavernous Region. Built around the Hidden River Cave from which Horse Cave received it's name, the community was in a valley completely surrounded by forested hills.

Horse Cave was a very unique place in which to live. The community had been electrically lighted since 1892 — the second town in the state to have that distinction. Perhaps even more importantly, the town was comprised of extraordinarily pleasant and friendly people.

By chance, while in Horse Cave, Charles met a lovely, dark-haired, young girl. She was standing on the sidewalk in front of the New York Cash Store. Upon parking his car in front of the store, the car backfired, startling her, causing her to drop some of her parcels. Charles quickly jumped out of his automobile, and ran to her and with his soft Southern drawl said, "I do beg your forgiveness." As he gathered her parcels, he asked, "Are you alright?"

The young girl laughed, and brushed her very long hair over her shoulders, and said, "Yes, I'm perfectly fine. I was just startled, that's all." As the boyish-looking Charles gazed upon the young girl he could not help but notice her exquisite features and beautiful brown eyes. Her raven colored long hair was not straight, yet not curly. She had an English rose, porcelain-like complexion. He thought to himself that he had never before in his life met anyone as lovely as she. For a moment, she had literally taken his breath away.

His thoughts were running rampart. He knew in his heart that she was someone he really wanted to know. While Charles was trying to think of something profound to say, he feared that he would say something that would cause her to make an excuse to eventually walk away.

The sun felt scorching! After what seemed to be an eternity, Charles finally said, "Forgive me for staring at you. My name is Charles Spencer. People call me, "Mr. Charlie." I'm a salesman from Madisonville. I sell salts."

The young girl curtsied ever so slightly and said, "Hello. My name is Lulu Lee." She smiled and seemed to be waiting for Charles to say something more. He finally complied and inquired, "Do you live in Horse Cave?"

Lulu Lee answered, "Yes, I do. I live with my parents just at the edge of town. We're the Taylors. I'm doing some shopping for my mother."

Charles could not help but notice that Lulu Lee was a petite young lady, with a waspish waist and ample bosom. Being a slight man, himself, as well as being on the shorter side, he felt she was perfect in every way. He wondered how many other men felt as he.

After several moments of exchanging pleasantries, there was a definite lull in the conversation. Charles knew he had to do or say something to keep her attention.

Finally, Charles said, "With all due respect, is it possible that I could assist you with your parcels, and perhaps give you a ride home in my automobile, whenever you are ready?"

Lulu Lee cast her eyes downward at first, and then gazed slightly up into his boyish flickering smile and vibrant blue eyes and said, "Oh, no thank you, Sir. That wouldn't be proper. My father would not look kindly upon you if you drove me home." Then giggling and tossing her hair, Lulu Lee added, "Besides, I rode to town on my bicycle."

Charles had never before been addressed as "Sir." He nervously wondered, if she thought him to be too old, to be conversing with him in such a manner. He did so want to keep her in conversation. Charles continued, "I'm eighteen years old, soon to be nineteen, and I work for our family business. I do hope one day to be in business for myself, maybe in a large city. I plan to travel and see the areas outside of Kentucky. I plan to have my own automobile someday, and that's when I'll really begin my travels."

Lulu Lee joined into the friendly exchange and said, "I plan to attend a business college in the near future. I just turned sixteen. I feel that it is time to make definite plans for a career."

Charles admired her forthrightness and commented, "I encourage you to do so. I respect your plans very much."

And then the moment finally came. Lulu Lee said, "I must be going. My mother will wonder why I am so tardy, if I linger any longer." With that said, she turned to get on her bicycle.

Charles quickly held the handlebars steady so that she could organize her parcels in the basket, sit on the seat, and arrange her flowing skirt; in essence, he was keeping the bicycle from moving away.

Their eyes looked searchingly and deeply at each other. Very spontaneously, Charles said, "Is it at all possible that I could see you again?"

Lulu Lee's eyes widened and smiling, she said, "When would you like to see me?" He did indeed like her forthrightness! Charles said, "I plan to return to Horse Cave in two weeks. Would that be a convenient time to see you again?"

Lulu Lee answered, "Oh yes. That would be nice." Hesitantly, she said, "Could we meet in two weeks from today, right here in front of the store, at two o'clock?'

Charles grinned and said, "Absolutely! I will look forward to it."

Lulu Lee started to pedal her bicycle, gave him a farewell glance, and waved to him as she rode off. Charles enthusiastically returned the gesture. Charles thought to himself, that he only hoped that nothing would stand in her way of meeting him in two weeks. He stood there and watched this very special and beautiful young lady, until she turned the corner, and he could no longer see her.

What Charles didn't know was just how special this young lady was! Lulu Lee had grand ancestry. Not only was she from a family of staunch Southern traditions, she was a third cousin to Jefferson Davis, who was a United States Senator, Secretary of War and eventually, President of the Confederacy. She was a distant cousin to the author, Louisa May Alcott, and by a cousin's marriage, to John Quincy Adams, sixth President of the United States. She was a product of true Southern heritage. Her lineage was indeed honorable!

Destination, Horse Cave

It was less than two weeks later when Charles left his family home in Madisonville to begin another selling trip with a destination of Horse Cave and to meet with Lulu Lee. He had anxiously looked forward to this day. Lulu Lee had been constantly on his mind.

Charles thought of several topics which he could converse with her, but as he thought them through, they all seemed so mundane. Having been offered this second opportunity to be with her, he wanted everything to be perfect!

Securing his salts in the trunk of the car, along with his personal suitcase, he placed an ice chest containing sandwiches, fruit, and a Thermos of iced tea on the seat next to him. It was Charles' plan not to lose any amount of time stopping for meals along the way; he wanted to stay ahead of his schedule.

Dressed in a suit, Charles placed his coat and necktie on the back seat, and began his journey driving southeast, with an itinerary of stopping in several small villages before arriving in Horse Cave. As he drove along the road, Charles gazed at the rolling manicured lawns of the plantations of his home state of Kentucky. Having the dream of owning his own business one day, he knew he would have to venture out of this beautiful state to broaden his sales contacts.

Ultimately, he wanted to settle down permanently in the bluegrass state of Kentucky. These were his roots.

Driving toward Drakesboro, Charles' thoughts were of Lulu Lee, and how he had met her only by chance. Now, just a few days later, he seemed to be planning his entire life around her. He kept telling himself that he had to take one day at a time, and not let his emotions run rampant in making plans that might never materialize. In the back of his mind though, Charles held the thought that Lulu Lee was from Kentucky, and surely she would be pleased to always live here, as well—with him.

Stopping in Drakesboro, before going on to Morgantown and Brownsville, Charles met his former clients, and made idle chatter as he secured his business deals. The businessmen of Drakesboro had always been kind to him. In the earlier days, when he was trying to establish himself, they had welcomed him and were always ready to listen to him. Now it was his turn to listen to them, whether it was about slow business, their health, or even the weather, over a glass of lemonade.

The next stop down the road was Morgantown. It was Charles' plan to complete his business transactions by the end of the day, so that after spending the night there, he would only have one more stop in Brownsville the next morning, before reaching Horse Cave.

Arriving in Morgantown that afternoon, Charles visited three businesses that always counted on him to keep them supplied with the salts. It was from one of these businesses, that he was bestowed the title, "Mr. Charlie," when he was just sixteen and beginning his career as a salesman. He appreciated their kindnesses and patience with him, and made it a point to tell them.

One of the gentlemen, Eden Rand, had taken him under his wing and guided him as to the direction in which his business should go. Eden insisted to Charles, that whenever he was in town, he should dine and stay with his family before venturing to the next town. It was rather an unwritten rule. Charles was very grateful, and regarded Eden as one of those friends for life. But Charles felt close to many of his clients; he was that sort of consummate businessman.

The last stop was Brownsville. Charles arose very early the next morning. He hadn't slept very well during the night, as his eagerness to reach Horse Cave was foremost on his mind. He entertained the thought that possibly Lulu Lee would not be there. Maybe by now, she had forgotten about their planned meeting that had been made in such haste. He worried about the possibility that Lulu Lee might have had a change of heart, or worse, her parents, had forbidden her to keep such an irresponsible encounter.

Declining breakfast, but enjoying a cup of coffee with Eden, he once again thanked him for his hospitality. Charles bade good-bye, and drove down the long driveway, and on to the main road to Brownsville. It was early in the day, yet he could see the heat rising on the road. With no wind to be felt, Charles knew that the day would soon become quite warm.

The drive to Brownsville seemed exceedingly long. Of the utmost importance, Charles knew that he could not linger long, or wile away the time at any of his appointments, as he usually did, or he would risk being late for his meeting with Lulu Lee at two o'clock.

Completing his business stops in Brownsville, Charles jumped into his car, and drove quickly down the road. Some of his friends noticed his quick departure, and shouted, "Charlie! What's the rush? Stay awhile!" Charles threw back his head, laughed pretentiously, waved fervently and drove away. He hoped he had not left the impression of being distant, but he was running late!

Charles arrived at the outskirts of Horse Cave just a few minutes past one o'clock. Glancing into a mirror to smooth over his wind-blown hair, he realized that he just had time to stop at the paint store to fill his car with petrol, as well as throw some water on his face, and change his shirt. It seemed to Charles, as though his life was hanging in the balance. He thought he just had to make a good impression. He only hoped that Lulu Lee was as eager to meet him, as he was to meet her.

Pulling up to the New York Cash Store where they had agreed to meet, Charles parked his automobile, and got out of the car to stand on the stoop of the store. In doing so,

Charles was afforded a better view of the street in both directions. His heart was racing.

His plan was to invite Lulu Lee to have lunch with him, and then to go for a walk in the Horse Cave City Park, or perhaps, even for a ride in his automobile. He so wanted to know her better. But for now, Lulu Lee was nowhere in sight. He wondered when, or if, she would arrive on her bicycle. Maybe all of his plans would go awry.

"Charlie! Charlie!"

He knew it was her voice, and turned around with a large grin on his face. With the sun in his eyes, he at first, did not see Lulu Lee driving up in a Duryea Motor Wagon. More importantly, he did not see the woman sitting next to Lulu Lee.

Charles approached her automobile, and with his hat in his hand, smiled and said, "Hello, Lulu Lee. I am so happy that you could keep our meeting."

Lulu Lee was unable to hide her excitement. "Charlie, it's so grand to see you again! Please meet my mother. I've told Mother and Dad all about you, and how we met! Mother, this is Charles Spencer. Charlie, this is my mother, Angeline Taylor."

Charles rushed to the other side of the automobile, and extended his hand to greet Mrs. Taylor. Charles could not help but notice that Mrs. Taylor's appearance was that of a strikingly handsome woman, although her face was half hidden under the wide brimmed hat that she wore.

"Hello, Mrs. Taylor," said Charles.

Mrs. Taylor replied, "Good afternoon, Charles. Welcome to Horse Cave. It's nice to meet you. Lulu Lee has told us of your meeting, a couple of weeks ago. I hope you had an uneventful drive to our town."

Charles noticed Mrs. Taylor presented herself with grace and dignity and possessed a soft voice. Before Charles could interject any words, Mrs. Taylor said, "If you care to do so, Lulu Lee and I would like to extend a warm invitation to you, to dine with our family this evening. We would especially like for you to come to our home, to meet Mr. Taylor, as well."

At first, Charles stuttered in getting his words out. He had not expected this. In fact, he wasn't even certain what he had expected! He just hadn't thought it through. "Gosh, I mean, how very thoughtful! I would be pleased to have dinner with your family!" said Charles. Still, Charles just wasn't certain how comfortable it would be to meet Lulu Lee's father so soon.

Angeline Taylor sensed the uneasiness in Charles' demeanor. Not wanting him to feel this discomfort, Angeline said, "Charles, Mr. Taylor and I have so looked forward to this day. If you will follow us, we will show you the way to our home."

Charles smiled at Lulu Lee. There was an unspoken communication between them. While Charles looked at Lulu Lee, hoping against all odds that he would do and say everything right, Lulu Lee gave him a big smile, and a small wink of her eye. With that gesture from her, an air of confidence came over him.

Welcome To Mulberry

Following Lulu Lee, as she drove to the Taylor home, Charles was very impressed that Lulu Lee was driving an automobile. It was most rare for a woman to drive a car, even more so, for a young girl. He smiled quietly to himself.

Within several minutes, the two cars drove up to a large brick, Colonial house. The four pillars on the front of the house, with a white fence surrounding the entire farm, indicated an air of opulence. A carpet of green grass fronted the beautiful home. A gentleman, who he presumed to be Lulu Lee's father, was in the front yard.

Mr. Taylor hastened to the automobile, to assist his wife and Lulu Lee. "Welcome home, Angeline! Lulu Lee, did the car handle alright?" Having assisted the ladies out of the automobile, Mr. Taylor walked over to Charles, extended his hand to him, and said, "Hello! I'm Winston Taylor. Welcome to Mulberry, our home. I've certainly heard a lot about you."

Lulu Lee's cheeks flushed. She wished her father hadn't said that, but the statement brought a smile to Charles' face.

With pleasantries exchanged, they all walked into the Taylor home. Looking around the room, Charles recognized the elements of grandeur as belonging to a very successful man. There were large ancestral portraits on the walls of the staircase, oversized crystal chandeliers hanging high above on the ceilings, and satin couches that complimented the very large parlors. Charles wondered to himself, "Just who were the Taylors?"

Mr. Taylor said, "Let us all get to know one another. Let's be seated here in our sunroom. This is my favorite room in the house. It's a perfect room for relaxation and conversation."

Enjoying a glass of iced tea, and a lively conversation of how Charles and Lulu Lee met, Mr. Taylor said, "Charles, tell me a little bit about your family. Lulu Lee has told us you sell salts. Tell me about that business." Mr. Taylor commented, "I am very impressed that your ancestors emigrated from England."

Charles said, "Some of my relatives that made the crossing with my grandparents chose to settle in New York and Palm Beach. My grandparents chose Kentucky, as my grandmother was a minister and had plans to preach in this state. I guess being a woman minister was unheard of in those days. But Kentucky, here we are!"

"Your grandfather was a wise man, Charles," said Mr. Taylor.

"As far as answering your questions about our salt business, Charles said, my grandfather discovered a salt lick in Dawson Springs and I guess that was the stimulus that brought him into the business. I shall always remember helping my grandfather in panning for mineral salts. I regard it as a special memory of my childhood."

"It seems to me that the business of salts is a good one," said Mr. Taylor, "but what are your plans for the future?"

When Charles mentioned, that his father felt it was time to expand the business outside of Kentucky, Mr. Taylor said, "I fail to comprehend why anyone would want to venture from Kentucky!"

During dinner, Charles was seated directly across the table from Lulu Lee. Through the light of the candles, Charles could see every expression on her face. The dinner conversation was very relaxed. Mr. Taylor spoke of his ancestry, and how he, himself, had lived in Horse Cave his entire life. He made it clear, that it was his fervent hope for his family, always, to remain on, and cultivate, Mulberry, the Taylor farm.

Charles could not help but wonder if perhaps, Mr. Taylor was driving home a point directed to him.

Changing the subject, Charles said to Mr. Taylor, "I know that the English people tend to name their homes, but why is your farm called Mulberry?"

Mr. Taylor deferred to Mrs. Taylor.

In a delightful way, Angeline told the story of how her mother taught her the song "Here We Go Round the Mulberry Bush." "It is just a fond memory that I don't want to forget," Mrs. Taylor said. "It is just a family endearment, Charles. It means a lot to me, I guess. So 'Mulberry' it is!"

After dinner, Mr. Taylor suggested he show Charles around the grounds before it turned dark, but Mrs. Taylor intervened. As protective as Mrs. Taylor was toward Lulu Lee, it was a surprise when Mrs. Taylor said, "Oh Winston, I do believe that the young folks can find their way around in the horse and buggy just fine by themselves."

Charles said, "What a delightful thing to do." Turning to Lulu Lee, Charles said, "I will have to watch my time, as my automobile's headlights do not cast much light, and it might turn out to be a challenging drive on unfamiliar roads back to the hotel where I plan to stay."

"Oh no!" exclaimed Lulu Lee, "Mother and Daddy are planning for you to stay with us. The guest room is already made up for you. Please plan to stay; then we will be able to visit longer. I had hoped that you would have an extended stay with us. Is that possible?"

Charles looked to Mr. And Mrs. Taylor for some sort of affirmation. Both smiled, and nodded in agreement. This was more than he had expected. Hesitantly, he graciously accepted the invitation.

A Proposal of Marriage

In the months to follow, an extraordinary romance blossomed between Lulu Lee and Charles. Charles returned again and again to the Taylor farm. Sometimes, he combined a selling trip with his visits, but for the most part, his trips to Horse Cave were to pursue Lulu Lee with determination and commitment.

There were times when Charles was visiting the Taylor family, when he felt Mr. Taylor was attempting to interest him in the ramifications of running the farm that primarily grew tobacco. Charles appeared to listen with interest even though he cared very little where the conversation was going.

However, when Winston Taylor talked about his champion racehorses and their care, Charles was particularly interested. Charles especially enjoyed hearing Mr. Taylor expound of various races that some of his horses had won. Charles always listened with enthusiasm, as owning horses was a far-away dream of his own, while owning and running a farm was not. Charles regarded himself as a salesman and that is where he was determined to stay. He was going to be a business tycoon one day!

Charles knew that eventually he would have to make this all very clear to Lulu Lee's family, and it might be at that time that Mr. and Mrs. Taylor would change their warm feelings toward him.

It was the Christmas season and Charles was spending part of the holidays with the Taylor family. Charles had known Lulu Lee only four months. One evening, while strolling around the grounds with Lulu Lee on the quiet field of new-fallen snow, he stopped and pulled her closer to him. The moonlight, reflecting from the snow, provided perfect lighting for her face as he gazed upon her.

"Lulu Lee, you must know that I have grown to love you very much. I know that I have never spoken these words to you before, but I tell you at this moment that I can't imagine living the rest of my life without you by my side." Before he gave her a chance to respond, he continued, "My future plans are to move north to Indiana. I have been offered a position as a salesman for a meat packing plant in Evansville, which my parents feel that I should accept. My younger brothers will be leading the way in our family salts business. While I do know that any man would be fortunate to have you for a wife, I fervently hope that you will consider going there with me. Please accept my proposal of marriage and come with me to start our new life."

Charles continued, "Lulu Lee, it would please me very much that you not give up on any of your own plans of entering a business college. I would never want to take away any of your own dreams."

Lulu Lee answered very emotionally, "Charlie, I do love you too. With all my heart, I do want to be your wife; but Charlie, you absolutely must ask my father for my hand in marriage first. Without his permission, we cannot marry. I will take it upon myself to speak to my mother."

Asking Mr. Taylor for permission to marry his daughter, as well as for both of her parents blessings, would be the next hurdle that Charles knew would be monumental. Lulu Lee and her mother had strong bonds between them, and he worried that her mother would be completely devastated with the prospect of her young daughter leaving the homestead, but even more importantly, leaving her Southern roots in Kentucky, to go north.

As was expected, when Lulu Lee spoke to her mother of her plans to marry Charles, Mrs. Taylor range of emotions was that of concern, fear and even anger, over the prospect of Lulu Lee leaving her family. Mrs. Taylor expressed to Lulu Lee, "My darling daughter, you are so young to make such a decision in your life. I say this especially because you have only known Charles for such a short time. Are you certain that he is the one with whom you want to spend the rest of your life? I implore you to come to your senses, think all this through and perhaps consider it later in life." She reached over to kiss Lulu Lee on her forehead and said, "Now let us have no more discussion about this matter."

While Charles preferred to think of Mrs. Taylor's reaction to his proposal of marriage to their daughter as something all mothers do when a daughter decides to leave home to marry, he could only wonder how Mr. Taylor would react. He hoped that he would not fall out of favor completely with this family.

Nervously speaking to Mr. Taylor for Lulu Lee's hand in marriage, Charles said. "Mr. Taylor, I have asked Lulu Lee for her hand in marriage. She has accepted my proposal, only if both of her parents will give us their blessings and permission to marry. Mr. Taylor, please know that Lulu Lee and I will have no financial difficulties, and only love, honor, and decency will prevail in our marriage." Charles also made it a point to speak of his dream to return to Kentucky one day.

The "returning to Kentucky one day" was the phrase that softened the fact that their daughter would be moving away from them. Winston Taylor even found promise in this young man and bestowed his blessings to both of the young people.

Never one to stand in opposition with Mr. Taylor, Angeline smiled through her tears, hugged the children and gave them her blessings as well—but with great reluctance. Angeline put forth a facade of graciousness, but in reality, she was extremely sad to have their daughter venture away from them. It seemed to Angeline that it was only a short time ago that their daughter was playing with her dolls and sitting on their laps.

The memories of Angeline being so proud to show Lulu Lee off to their political friends and relatives; as well as the galas and picnics at Mulberry where their daughter was always the star attraction, was now going to be a thing of the past. Angeline was not certain that she could rise to this challenge!

It was very obvious that Winston and Angeline Taylor were not really ready to relinquish their sixteen-year old daughter to this young man. Angeline also knew that without Lulu Lee, her own life would become an emotional blur. Grieving for the closeness of their young daughter would certainly take a toll on both of her parents.

Southern Heritage

Angeline Taylor had known sadness for much of her life. She was familiar with tragedy interrupting happiness. As a young girl, she had previously been married, to a Confederate soldier, who subsequently was killed in the Civil War during a battle nine miles outside of Nashville. It had been a marriage of short duration, before he went to war. Angeline had been a young widow, left with two young sons.

November 18, 1862
Camp Stone River Near Edgefield, Tennessee

My Dear Wife, Angeline,

I am taking this privilege of writing to you a few lines to inform you that at present, I am well and enjoying health as best as can be expected. I suppose this letter will have an opportunity of reaching you and I am hoping you are well and will keep in good health until I reach home again and I hope that will be about Spring.

It is most horrible to say to you that there was a very large battle fought at Nashville some few days ago, which was a daring fight. We put forth to Edgefield where we were firing into the Yankees. We had a large force to take Nashville but we found ourselves at the end of the horn and it was not in our power to do so. We had to retreat for nine or ten miles.

Hundreds of our men were slain and as many wounded. Four or five hundred men have been taken prisoner. I did manage to escape. I am at the moment about nine miles from the great city of Nashville. We expect another attack very soon. I should be very glad to receive a letter from you very soon so as to learn how you are getting along. The last letter that I received from you was dated November 10th You said the property and the farm were all right. Now my dear wife, it is with kindness that I issue such open thoughts as I am going to do. Take care of everything that is around you and I hope you will get along until I return home again to you and when we will smile once more. Then we will live together with lovingness and kindness forever and ever. Please hug the children for me.

I remain your kind husband now and in the future.

William

(Someone wrote this note on the envelope: This letter was found on the body of this soldier. He had been shot through the chest and head.)

Devastated, lonely, and fearful with the prospects of the Yankees returning to Horse Cave, Angeline hid her silver and what money she had, by burying them in the ground. She spent long hours in the fields cultivating the crops which supplied her food. At times, she felt she could not continue to live, knowing her husband would never return. In Angeline's mind, the future for her was empty.

In the course of time, Angeline did remarry, but this marriage too was short-lived. Tragedy struck again, when her second husband was fatally stabbed during a card game in a tavern in Horse Cave. A daughter, Jennie and a son, George, had been born to this marriage, ultimately making them half-siblings to the earlier born children and a half sister to the eventual Lulu Lee.

While still a young widow of 28 years old Angeline was married for the third time, to her present husband, Winston Jones Taylor. Winston had promised Angeline that he would do everything within his power to assure her and the children of a life of comfort. They were overjoyed when Angeline gave birth to their adorable baby daughter, Lulu Lee, in 1882.

———————

At the time of Charlie's proposal to Lulu Lee, her sister, Jennie was thirteen years older and was married and living in New Orleans. The two girls, writing to each other weekly, had always exhibited a strong bond between them. Now Angeline and Winston were entering a new phase of their lives, with losing their youngest daughter and last child to marriage so unexpectedly. They both knew having Lulu Lee move away from them would be an extreme hardship for both of them to endure.

Trying to console one another, they both acknowledged to each other that they did in fact like this young and ambitious Charles. They recognized that Charles seemed to be a young man of strict integrity with a splendid character and high ideals. They were also immensely heartened by Lulu Lee's show of affection for Charles and he for her. Despite their sadness that was so encompassing, they allowed their daughter to make her own decisions in this matter. They assured her that they would not try to dissuade her as difficult as all this was!

A matter that did concern Winston Taylor caused him to look at his wife and say, "Why would anyone want to leave Kentucky?"

Lives Change

As hurtful as moving to Indiana would be to Mr. and Mrs. Taylor, Charles realized that a change in his career was an absolute necessity, as the salts business was diminishing. People were discovering newer and better remedies for their ailments.

Accepting a sales position with the meat packing plant in Evansville, Charles felt that this move was a positive one, with good potential for advancement. His own family encouraged Charles in this direction, as they felt that this would also be a great opportunity for Charles to learn a new trade.

Charles Spencer's younger brothers, Albert and Frederick, who were still panning and selling salts for the family business in Dawson Springs, were excited for him to accept this newly offered position. It was their plan to join him in business one day. Charles had always wanted to be in business with his two brothers. As young lads, they had always talked of this dream. Their plans were almost a reality.

Angeline was pleased to know of Lulu Lee's future plans to enter a business college in Evansville, Indiana, after her marriage to Charles. Always a strong believer in women's rights, Angeline felt it to be important that Lulu Lee have a degree of independence. Having previously taught Lulu Lee to drive their motor car, a rather rare thing for a young lady to do at the turn of the century, Angeline was pleased that her daughter, again, would be ahead of her time.

With their lives now facing change, Angeline and Winston Taylor reluctantly moved forward with their young daughter's wedding plans. The last thing that they desired was for Lulu Lee to know was how very sad they felt and how very lost they would be without her.

Previously projecting herself as a social activist, Angeline found that now those things were not of importance to her. Her social clubs in Horse Cave were no longer a priority in her life. With a somber mood taking over her life, she was experiencing a severe depression-like state of mind. Solitude was what she preferred.

The Wedding

February 4, 1899. It was Lulu Lee Taylor's and Charles Spencer's wedding day! Only six months ago, sixteen-year-old Lulu Lee, and nineteen-year-old Charles had met in front of the New York Cash Store. What Angeline Taylor had previously called a "sweet whirl-wind" romance was now leading to a wedding ceremony assuming epic proportions, to be performed at Mulberry. Many area and state dignitaries had been invited and had traveled long distances to be a part of this prestigious event.

Lulu Lee's sister, Jennie was her only bridesmaid. Her three older brothers assisted in greeting the guests and guiding them to their seats. Dressed in a maroon taffeta, long sleeved bustled gown with crystal beading, and holding a bouquet of pink roses and baby's breath, Jennie looked as lovely as any bridesmaid possibly could. While many guests complimented Jennie on her loveliness, Jennie could be heard boasting ecstatically to all, "Wait until you see my very beautiful little sister." The loving bonds between the two sisters were very evident.

Conversely, Angeline was upstairs in her bedroom feeling very solemn. It was necessary for one of the servants to assist her in dressing. Angeline was attired in a pink lace gown, adorned with several long strands of pearls.

Angeline was aware that it was almost time to greet all of the guests already congregating downstairs.

Earlier in the day, she had had a long discussion with Lulu Lee, as to whether she was having any second thoughts about going through with this wedding, stating that everyone would understand, should she want to postpone this event.

Still holding out her own thoughts, Angeline walked across the hall to where Lulu Lee was finishing dressing. She asked again, "Lulu Lee, darling, remember if you are having any thoughts about canceling your wedding day, we could have one big party in lieu of the ceremony. I promise you, everyone would understand completely."

Lulu Lee hugged her mother and said, "Oh Mama, know that I love you and Poppa so very much, but I also love Charlie too. Please don't be sad. Mama, I hope that you and Poppa will visit us often, as we will visit both of you. Mama, before you know it, we'll be moving back to Kentucky! We promise you that! As Poppa has always said, 'Who would ever want to move away from Kentucky?'

With that said, Angeline took one last look at her fragile self in the large petticoat mirror, pinched her cheeks for color, and put on her best gracious smile. Descending the grand stairs, Angeline extended her hand to her guests and said, "Isn't this a grand occasion? Thank you for coming!"

And all too soon, the sound of the music, *Ave Maria*, a favorite hymn loved by Lulu Lee, was being played on the harpsichord. The prelude before *The Wedding March* was the signal that the moment of the wedding was about to begin. It was time for everyone to be seated. Angeline composed herself and accepted that soon she would be "the mother of the bride."

Jennie had been correct. Lulu Lee was an astonishingly beautiful bride. Her long dark hair was styled in an upsweep, away from her face, emphasizing her dark brown eyes and high cheekbones. Her satin gown, bought in Cincinnati, had a form fitting waist and a voluminous skirt. She wore a coif with an illusion veil with seed pearls in abundance. Lulu Lee was radiant as she entered the room on the arm of her father as the wedding music began.

Lulu Lee and Charles appeared confident, calm and much in love, as they stood before the minister. They made an extraordinarily striking couple, and no one was hesitant in mentioning it. As Lulu Lee and Charles gazed into each other's eyes, they vaguely heard the minister say, "Let no man put asunder." What they did hear most clearly was, "Ladies and gentlemen, I now present to you, Mr. and Mrs. Charles Robinson Spencer."

Lulu Lee and Charles were so elated and so in love. They both knew "no man could put asunder." Theirs was a true and forever marriage. Winston Taylor squeezed his wife's arm, while Angeline tried inconspicuously to dab the tears, welling in her eyes.

After the ceremony and union of their hearts was solemnized, Charles took his beautiful bride's arm tenderly in his, and escorted her around the parlor to greet each and every wedding guest. It was important to the couple that they thank everyone for coming to their wedding. Charles boasted to all that Lulu Lee would always be his first priority.

With a special toast, he assured his bride, in front of all of their guests, that she would always have his love and devotion. Charles said, "Lulu Lee, I will cherish you, forever!"

The guests were feted with a lavish reception around an oversized dining table with crystal candelabras on each side of the six-tiered wedding cake. Champagne flowed abundantly for the guests. Following the reception and dinner, an evening of dancing in the lofty ceiling ballroom afforded all a wonderful evening.

While the Spencer and the Taylor family members exchanged nervous pleasantries, assuring one another that their young children would fare successfully in their lives as man and wife, the young couple tried to convince everyone that they were fully aware of the responsibilities of marriage.

And all too soon, fireworks were set off in the skies signifying that the evening was coming to an end. The many guests started to depart, but not before they congratulated the newlyweds again, giving them their best wishes for a blissful and blessed wedded life.

Again, the guests thanked Angeline and Winston for a spectacular and exciting day. Since it was known that it would be a very late evening, Charlie's family and both sets of parents, and grandparents had previously been invited to spend the night at Mulberry. The newlyweds were to stay in the farm's guesthouse. The end of a day that Angeline had not wanted to come had ended.

————————

The following morning, Winston and Angeline Taylor entertained the new relatives, with a breakfast in honor of the bride and groom. Sitting around various tables, everyone, wanting to get to know one another better, delighted in exchanging stories of their prideful heritage.

Then, all too soon, it was time for Lulu Lee and Charles, to bid farewell to their parents. After much last-minute teary conversation, with words of advice for Lulu Lee and Charles, and embraces, Charles and Lulu Lee said their goodbyes.

Once again, Charles assured the Taylor family members that he would provide a good home for his bride. Having said that, Charles and Lulu Lee again hugged everyone goodbye and drove down the driveway to start their journey to Evansville. Looking back and waving enthusiastically to her parents, Lulu Lee shouted, "Thank you, Mama! Don't worry, Poppa! I love you both!" Angeline and Winston Taylor knew that they had to accept a new life.

A New Beginning

Lulu Lee and Charles found a small and picturesque home on the outskirts of Evansville. They found it exciting living near the big city, while leading an idyllic life in the country with gardens and greenery. In the back of their minds though they both realized it was different from their roots in Kentucky. Charles made friends easily at the meat packing plant. His rugged honesty and loyalty to his co-workers and employer put him on everyone's social list. He and Lulu Lee were afforded the best of opportunities to meet people. Charles enjoyed being a salesman in this new line of work, and proved early to be a credit to his company. Things seemed almost too perfect!

While Lulu Lee waited for the fall semester to begin at the Evansville Business College, she tried to stay busy creating a home for Charlie. She was so happy over having been accepted into college, and especially excited having breeched a man's world. She knew her mother would be proud.

But in spite of all the pieces of her new life starting to come together, Lulu Lee was lonely and feeling very sad. She seemed to cry easily. She was tired and at times even nauseated. Lulu Lee surmised that being in a strange place, away from her family, that she had given into homesickness.

But fate sometimes has a way of making life's decisions. With Charles' insistence that he take her to a doctor, Lulu

Lee found out that she would soon be having a baby in late November.

There were many mixed emotions. While Charles was very excited, Lulu Lee wasn't certain how she felt. Her world was taking an unexpected turn. What about her schooling? What about her mother's expectations for her? She wanted to go home. The young Lulu Lee sat down, and immediately penned a letter to her mother, hoping she would say, "Come home!"

Angeline wrote, "Darling, we are so excited for all of us! Of course we want to be with you for the arrival of the new addition to our family. Do not even think about schooling for now. You are very young, and there will be a perfect time for you to attend school. Poppa and I will come to Evansville for Thanksgiving, and will stay on through the Christmas holidays, so that we may assist you, in every way. Our baby is the most important thing to be thinking about now."

Lulu Lee thought her mother made it all sound so wonderful. Now Lulu Lee too, felt excited just thinking about the arrival of their first child. Would it be a boy? Would it be a girl? She knew in her heart, that if she had a baby girl, she would name the baby, Angeline, after her mother.

Charles too, was getting into the mode of awaiting and wondering about the new baby. He pictured himself holding his son in his arms; yet, he thought a baby girl would be so wonderful too. They could name her after his mother, Ida.

It was a lovely fall, October morning. While Charles was away at the meat plant, Lulu Lee decided to go for a short ride with her horse, Lolly. Lolly had been Lulu Lee's horse since she was seven years old. She was the most gentle of all the horses that Mr. Taylor had ever owned. Mr. Taylor knew how much his daughter loved her horse, and how sad she had been to leave her behind. When she moved to Evansville, he had made arrangements to send Lolly to her.

Lulu Lee had been especially thrilled that she could pasture Lolly directly behind their home, along with other horses. It was also a convenient place as well, when it was time for her to groom Lolly or just be with her horse.

Lulu Lee hitched Lolly to her buggy, and trotted her horse on the country lane behind their home. A short time into the ride, a rabbit ran across Lolly's path causing her to spook. Lulu Lee was thrown from side to side in the buggy, as she tightly held the reins. Lulu Lee screamed, "No Lolly! No Lolly! Whoa! Good girl." Lulu Lee tried to calm herself, and the horse. Although shaken, Lulu Lee was able to bring Lolly under control, and they continued their ride.

It was only upon arriving home, did Lulu Lee fear that something was really wrong. Her baby, inside of her, seemed to be moving an unusual amount. A cramping sensation came over her. She feared that Charlie would not be home for several hours, so she decided to lay upon her bed, with hopes of stopping whatever was happening to her. Lulu Lee was not certain what happened, but either she fell asleep or she fell into an unconscious state.

———————

The next thing Lulu Lee realized, Charlie was standing over her. Charlie was pleading, "Lulu Lee, Lulu Lee. Please open your eyes! I've summoned the doctor and he is on his way! Try to hold on, darling."

Lulu Lee was in such discomfort. She smiled weakly, and tried to assure Charlie that she was all right. Again, she fell into a deep sleep.

That evening, a baby girl was born prematurely to Lulu Lee at their home. Subsequently, the wonderful news of the arrival of their tiny baby daughter was diminished, when Lulu Lee and Charles were told by the doctor that there would not be any possibility, of future babies. Lulu Lee, silently thanked God for at least giving them this one adorable, sweet, little baby girl.

The doctor surmised that the newly born baby girl only weighed about a pound and a half. She was placed in a shoebox, and swaddled in cotton to keep warm. The baby's low weight was a definite threat to survival. The doctor commented that the baby's heart was somewhat on the weak side, but his encouraging remarks, "This baby has strong lungs. She is spirited and she is a survivor! You'll see!" offered much hope to the new parents.

Charles telephoned both sets of parents, as well as her sister, Jennie in New Orleans, telling them of the arrival of their baby daughter, Ida Angeline. Mrs. Taylor was thrilled beyond words and told Charles that they would get on the road immediately. Angeline could not wait to meet her namesake.

Upon telling his parents, Ida and John, Mrs. Spencer said, "Oh Charlie, I couldn't be more pleased. Thank you so much for the honor of naming the baby after me. We will drive immediately to meet my namesake. See you soon!"

———————

With much love and constant attention, little Ida Angeline, named in honor of both grandmothers, would claim her spot in the Spencer family!

———————

Little Ida Angeline was the center of her adoring relatives' world. She was considered to be a miracle baby—very special! Lulu Lee and Charles were determined to bestow as much love and attention as possible upon their new baby. They felt very blessed that she had entered their world. As a result, Little Ida Angeline was coddled and pampered: and she held everyone's full attention at all times.

Since the baby was constantly being called "Ida" by one set of grandparents, and "Angeline"' by the other set of grandparents, Lulu Lee and Charles combined both names, and proudly named her, 'Idalynn.'

In spite of all that was done to care for little Idalynn, she was a weak child. Whether not allowed, or not able, Idalynn did not walk until she was three years old. When the child was stricken with smallpox at two years of age the circle of protectiveness drew even closer. Lulu Lee felt their only purpose in life now, was to love and protect, and always be there for their baby.

Lulu Lee was a good mother to little Idalynn. While Charles was continuing to excel with his career as a productive and confident salesman, Lulu Lee was enjoying her life at home with Idalynn. It was just like playing dolls. At times, Lulu Lee would hitch her horse, Lolly, to a buggy, and off they would go for a jaunt to see and meet many of the people in town. Lulu Lee's thoughts and aspirations of attending a business college now seemed to be far away, in a past life.

The Best of Circumstances/
The worst of Times

Charles possessed the winning combination of ability and deep respect from his peers. His personal connections with powerful businessmen afforded him valuable opportunities, and the young Charles Spencer family was bestowed a place in Evansville's high society, receiving all of the best of invitations offered.

Within a few years, Charles, Lulu Lee, and little Idalynn moved to a very prestigious neighborhood in Evansville. This move was important to Charles. His philosophy was to be on the same or better social standing as his clients. Their large, two-story, brick Colonial home had eight massive columns across the front of the house. To each side of the front walk were two stone structures engraved with the name, Mulberry—Lulu Lee's wish for her home's name.

Maids were employed in the home, not only to ensure that the home was run properly, but also to permit Lulu Lee time to meet with the most prominent women in town, and be a part of the best social circles. Lulu Lee insisted that a governess was always to be in attendance to watch over her small daughter should she find it necessary to be away from home. Little Idalynn was being raised in the best of circumstances.

In most respects, this Mulberry mirrored the home in which Lulu Lee had been raised. The massive chandeliers, the satin couches, the pictures hung along the staircase, all suggested a stately home. Charlie was proud of the home that Lulu Lee had put together. He wanted a Mulberry too! Not only did Lulu Lee emulate Mulberry, her agenda now, was to work tirelessly with charities, and women's causes—just like her mother had done.

Lulu Lee and Charles happily opened their home to their relatives. They encouraged visitors often. Lulu Lee's sister, Jennie and her husband Jared, were immensely proud to be connected to this wonderful couple.

Angeline Taylor couldn't have been more pleased! She couldn't even relate to the days when she had not wanted the marriage between her daughter and Charles to take place.

———

Through the ensuing years, Idalynn was groomed and dressed exquisitely. She took dancing, elocution, piano and equestrian instructions. She rode to school in a chauffeur-driven car, at all times protected. Although various servants attended to Idalynn, Lulu Lee was always a "hands-on" mother.

Idalynn was a charmer and Charles was particularly susceptible to her. She shared so much laughter with her father. When gifts were bestowed upon her, Charles would whisper in her ear, "Remember, you don't have to share!" Responding to all her requests, her desires were always met by those in attendance.

At a very young age, Idalynn had the ability, to hold everyone's attention, appearing to talk on any level, about any subject. What she didn't know, she made up. After all, her father had said to her, "Remember, you are special! You don't owe anybody, anything. Keep them guessing."

———————

The years passed quickly, and it seemed that everyone in the family had found their own successes. Charles was an outstanding member of the business world, serving on several boards, and was well on his way to being the business tycoon, to which he had always aspired. Lulu Lee was inducted into prestigious organizations, such as the Eastern Star, and Daughters of the Confederacy and Idalynn was immensely popular in school. She was never overlooked on anyone's invitation list.

When Idalynn turned sixteen, the free-spirited and diminutive, five-foot Idalynn was given a shiny black Ford, the "Tin Lizzie." She was the envy of all of her friends.

Though she did not know how to drive, then, or ever, it was what she wanted! Of course her wish was granted! Lulu Lee was inclined to believe that by giving her a car, she would surely want to learn to drive it. After all, Lulu Lee, herself, remembers being her age, and being so anxious to learn to drive. It was accepted as a step toward independence which Grandmother Taylor would insist, was appropriate for women.

Idalynn, however, preferred to have her friends drive her in her car. Her rational was, "Was this not what her chauffeurs had always done for her?" In time, this attitude would carry a heavy price.

Idalynn was turning into a "Flapper". These were fast times. With her bobbed hair, hiked-up skirts, and rolled down hose, exposing the rouge on her knees, Idalynn attended wild parties and had untamed friends. Idalynn was a young woman who was extreme in dress and speech, and was fearless of society's rules. She refused regimentation. To her, life was an adventurous game. Idalynn just didn't know how to play it.

One evening, after a round of parties, Idalynn and a carload of friends, were riding home in her car. Idalynn's escort, Danny was behind the wheel. As they were driving on a lonely winding road, laughing at one another's remarks, Ralph who was riding in the back seat with his girl friend, Mary Ann, noticed a train in the distance approaching the crossing ahead.

Ralph said, "Hey, Danny! Think you can put your pedal down and beat that train? Try it!"

Danny retorted, "No problem here. Hang on folks! Here we go!"

Mary Ann screamed, "No, Danny! Don't!

Idalynn shouted, "Do it Danny! Do it!"

The sounds of the crunching metal and steel of the Model T's head-on collision with the train, along with the screams of the car's passengers quieting down to moans, was evidence of a grave tragedy in play.

Having been thrown through the front windshield, Idalynn appeared to be lifeless on the side of the road for what seemed to be an eternity. One of the conductors on the train was able to summons help. Eventually, the ambulances arrived and took all four of the teenagers to the hospital.

Idalynn's classmate, Mary Ann, who had been riding in the backseat of the car, was dead upon arrival at the hospital. Her escort, Ralph, in the back seat with her, was the only person in the car who remained unscathed, and later told the police of the events leading up to the accident. Danny was not expected to live.

Along with many internal injuries, Idalynn's head had been severely gashed. Her face and forehead were torn open by shards of glass, while the status of her eyesight would remain questionable.

Lulu Lee and Charles were at home that evening, waiting for Idalynn to return with her friends. When the telephone call from the hospital came through to them, with the message that all parents dread to hear, both prepared to rush to her side, fearing their world, their reason for existence, was about to be taken from them. Charles prayed silently while the tears ran down his face. Lulu Lee sobbed hysterically.

Arriving at the hospital, the doctor spoke to Lulu Lee and Charles, "The gravity of your daughter's condition is critical. She is in a great deal of discomfort. Along with internal injuries, she has some deep facial lacerations, as well as injuries to the shoulder, pelvis and rib areas. For now, the best we can hope for is her survival. Saving her eyesight will be questionable for many weeks. I fear her sight might be severely compromised."

Charles was most impatient with the doctor's ambivalent words such as, "most likely", "the best we can hope for," and the word, "compromised." His intent was to seek the best of surgeons in the area and state to come immediately to his daughter's aid.

Surgeries followed surgeries. The days turned to weeks, the weeks turned to months, and still, there was little improvement. Lulu Lee refused to leave Idalynn's bedside. Idalynn's recuperation was extremely slow.

It was during this time that Lulu Lee said to Charles, "I want to leave the Evansville area. I do not want Idalynn to have access to the friends that she has chosen." Lulu Lee continued, "I beg you, Charles, wherever you choose to go, Idalynn and I will follow, just as soon as our daughter is able."

Arduous medical care, as well as good fortune, made it possible for Idalynn to walk away from this past horrendous ordeal with only slight facial scarring. However, the memory of her escort, Danny, dying, would be with her forever. As the doctor had predicted, Idalynn did have poor eyesight for the rest of her life.

Lulu Lee wanted their daughter to have a fresh start in life with new friends and surroundings at school. It was apparent that boundaries needed to be established, in order to rid Idalynn of her self-destructive behavior. To Lulu Lee, it was most important to change Idalynn's questionable reputation which was anything but pristine.

Though Charles' employer and their friends begged the couple to reconsider and stay in Evansville, Lulu Lee knew that even their dearest friends did not recognize the intense amount of emotional difficulty they were going through with their daughter. There was a time when Idalynn had been sweet and considerate; now she was dismissive and surly.

While Idalynn professed, "Mother, I don't know how all this could possibly have happened," Lulu Lee recognized, that Idalynn had a self-imposed detachment that she brought into play when she chose to believe certain things that happened, didn't happen. When things seemed out of control, Idalynn reverted to living in a fantasy world away from reality. More importantly, Lulu Lee recognized that she was Idalynn's enabler.

Still, Lulu Lee implored Charles to be patient with Idalynn, who seemed not to show any remorse by this accident. She appeared to take little responsibility for her own misbehavior. Idalynn glibly rationalized that Danny, who had been driving, was solely to blame.

Changing Directions

After many discussions with Lulu Lee, Charles decided that they should move to St. Louis. They would be closer to his brothers, who at this time were employed in the meat packing businesses, and Charles could possibly gain employment as well. For the present, Albert was working at Krey Packing Company, and Frederick was with Swift and Company.

While Charles decided to join Frederick at Swift and Company, the three Spencer brothers were elated, being in the same city with intermingling careers. The brotherly bonds were evident to all. Charles, confident with his salesmanship abilities, knew it would only be a matter of time before he would be looked upon favorably for advancement.

Lulu Lee and Idalynn were able to join Charles within a few weeks. The home they moved to in St. Louis dimmed in comparison to their Evansville home, but Lulu Lee was thrilled to be moving on to a new beginning. Whatever the future held, she would accept it with determination to once again find their place in society, which was so important to her and Charles. In the back of her mind though, she was haunted by the thought that by leaving Evansville they had in fact, moved further away from Horse Cave.

It was December 1915. Idalynn was almost seventeen years old and enrolled in high school. Lulu Lee was preparing for the holiday festivities when she received a telephone call from her father, telling her that her mother was gravely ill. Mr. Taylor said, "Lulu Lee, I think it is important that you come as soon as you are able. Your sister is also on her way here."

Lulu Lee immediately prepared to go to Horse Cave. Charles insisted that he accompany her on her journey, but Lulu Lee told Charles that she was perfectly able to make this trip alone. She reminded Charles that he needed to remain at home to be in charge of their home—and more importantly, Idalynn.

Upon arriving at her family home, Mulberry, Lulu Lee was advised that her mother did not have long to live. Lulu Lee phoned Charles to tell him that she needed to stay at her mother's side until death came to her.

It was while Lulu Lee and Jennie sat at their mother's bedside, that they listened to her recall her own life's stories of her girlhood, and growing up in Horse Cave. Angeline's stories reminded Lulu Lee of her own heritage in Kentucky. Now more than ever, Lulu Lee felt that she needed to return her own family to Kentucky; after all, this was where Charles belonged as well.

Angeline shared with her daughters, "It has always been my dream, that both of my daughters would one day return to Kentucky. I have always held out hope that at least one of my daughters would choose to come home to Mulberry so that our family home could live on."

Looking about the family home, Lulu Lee was reminded of the time when she was a child of about seven years old, that President Jefferson Davis visited their home, and held her on his lap and told tell her wonderful stories about the South. Lulu Lee felt a sense of aliveness, when thinking about her previous young life in Horse Cave. A flood of childhood memories had been triggered. She promised her mother, just moments before her passing on December 15th, "Mother, Charles and I will return home to Kentucky, just as soon as we can arrange it. I promise you that."

Charles showed great compassion to Lulu Lee when they all attended the funeral of her mother. For Lulu Lee, the loss of her mother meant a loss of a part of herself. She revered the stories that her mother had shared with her, and knew that those stories would keep her mother forever alive in her heart.

In the meantime, her profound grief stayed with her for such a long time that, at times, she felt it would never end. Trying to overcome her sorrows, she held hopes, dreams, and a mindset of moving her family home to Horse Cave.

Lulu Lee's sister, Jennie, had no children, so she insisted to Lulu Lee, that she and her husband could stay on for a while with their father at Mulberry, to assist him in adjusting to a life without Angeline. Lulu Lee could not have been more pleased. She thanked her sister profoundly, and promised Jennie that they would visit them often.

Returning home to St. Louis, Idalynn, Charles and Lulu Lee had a very somber holiday season. During one of their quiet evenings at home, Lulu Lee said, "Charlie, would you ever consider moving back to Horse Cave someday?"

Charles was surprised by this sudden suggestion of hers and said, "Lulu Lee, that is not even feasible, nor is it a possibility!" Hearing such an uncompromising remark from Charles, Lulu Lee said, "I do implore you, Charlie. Won't you give it some thought? My heart is aching to return to Kentucky."

———————

After several serious discussions with Lulu Lee over the ensuing weeks, Charles said, he understood her deep affinity with her thoughts of returning to Horse Cave, living close to her father to assist with his care, but Charles wanted Lulu Lee to understand that the family's living conditions would suffer if they were to relocate again, so soon.

As fate would play out, within a few weeks, Lulu Lee's sister, Jennie, called to inform Charles and Lulu Lee of their intensions to remain at Mulberry permanently. Jennie felt that their father needed someone to look after him. She did not want to leave him alone. Jennie wanted to know Lulu Lee's feelings about those plans.

Lulu Lee told her sister, "I couldn't be more pleased. I wholeheartedly agree that you both should continue to make Mulberry your home." Lulu Lee silently thought to herself, "I wish it were me that were going home to Mulberry.

Kentucky Plans Begin

Always remembering his vow to Lulu Lee to care for her and grant her any desires, Charles made plans to move his family back to Kentucky. Trying to suppress any doubts that he might have about this move, Charles rationalized that it was time to be closer to his parents, as well. In this manner he would be able to see them on a more frequent basis.

In the back of Lulu Lee's mind, however, were thoughts that soon it would be time for Idalynn to make her debut as a debutante, and in Lulu Lee's mind, to be a Southern debutante is what Lulu Lee wanted for Idalynn.

Always accepting any opportunity to make his daughter's welfare his priority, Charles agreed, once again, to change jobs. Charles thought that whatever Lulu Lee thought was best for Idalynn, would certainly be best for all of them.

Knowing it would be ideal for their daughter to walk the carefully-chosen path of a Lexington debutante, rather than being identified as a small town girl from Horse Cave, was the deciding factor to move.

Visiting Lexington, Lulu Lee was thrilled to see that it was a bustling and prosperous town of the early 1900's. Along with an opera house, libraries, and many churches, the University of Kentucky had been established. The University offered great sources for social activities and meeting intellectual friends. The Junior League, an organization promoting women's volunteerism, would also be an additional enticement for moving.

Lulu Lee was also pleased to see all the stately mansions that were built, as well as the city's planning for the building of other grand homes in the area. She was absolutely positive that moving to Lexington was the right direction in which to go.

With the move to Kentucky in the immediate plans, the ambitious Charles called his brothers to tell them of his idea to open a meat packing plant in Lexington. He wanted his brothers to join him in business. Charles offered to provide the financing.

Convincing his brothers to join him in this new venture was easily done, as the idea of working together had always been the ultimate goal of the three brothers. The younger brothers were excited with the idea of being in business with their older brother, and all agreed, Lexington would be the city for the best possibility of success. It was unanimous that Charles would be President of Spencer Brothers, Inc.

All the families were happy to be returning to their roots—Lulu Lee, especially so! However, Lulu Lee could not help but worry about the possibilities of failure with Charles' new business. What excuse could she offer to avail herself of any consequences of her persistence in moving back to Kentucky?

———————————

In Charles' fashion, failure was not to be the case. The Spencer Brothers Meat Packing Business was established on the northeast corner of Merino and West Vine Street in 1917. The brothers decided to buy up several blocks of homes near the plant, so their employees would have adequate and convenient housing. Appreciating all the employment opportunities afforded to their city, as well as their benevolences to their workers, the Spencer brothers were well-liked and well-respected in Lexington. The newly established meat plant appeared to offer a positive future for many people.

Charles, Albert and Frederick Spencer promoted themselves socially and acquired reputations of being some of Lexington's great benefactors. Once again, Charles was known as, "Mr. Charlie" by those who worked for, or knew him. Lexington was good to "Mr. Charlie." Without a doubt, "Mr. Charlie" was good to Lexington. Many times, it was inferred that Charles was "Mr. Lexington"! Charles had become an assertive and industrious business tycoon!

Ultimately, in 1924, the brothers were able to purchase a second meat plant on the Old Frankfort Pike on the L and N Railroad site.

A Gracious Way of Life

Charles, Lulu Lee and daughter, Idalynn moved into a magnificent colonial home on Versailles Parkway, three blocks east of Wilson Avenue. Again, the massive white pillars were a signature belonging to Charles and Lulu Lee Spencer. The decor of the home once again resembled the home in which Lulu Lee had lived as a young girl. It was becoming apparent that wherever Lulu Lee went, Mulberry followed.

The two-story colonial house had a wide center hall, with French doors leading to connecting rooms with tall ceilings and beautiful chandeliers throughout. The house had wrap-around porches, both upstairs and downstairs. The maroon carpeting and massive furniture presented an atmosphere of luxury and warmth.

Lulu Lee especially enjoyed the baby grand piano placed in the parlor. She could play by ear, any song requested of her. They were living a gracious way of life. Once again, Lulu Lee and Charles found their place in Lexington society.

Over the years, Charles' love and interest of horses never diminished. At this time in his life, he was able to indulge himself in his hobby of horses. On their family estate, Charles had built stables for the horses, not only for the very special and aged "Lolly," but for housing and training racehorses.

Charles made it a point to hire the best of horse trainers available. How he loved to arise each morning and walk to the stables and talk to the staff to discuss the training methods! He loved to question the trainers, in regard to the romance of the thoroughbred, and he constantly wanted to know whether he had any viable contenders for the various races. He loved this part of his existence. He was proud of his champions. Charles' lifestyle imitated art. It couldn't be matched in this city! He was a happy man!

Idalynn was living a fairy tale existence. With being a debutante, she was honored with several coming-out parties. The Lexington Herald Leader's society column wrote: "The diminutive Idalynn Spencer is this year's most elegant debutante, with a dazzlingly, yet understated charm and style. Miss Spencer exemplifies a true Southern Belle."

Lulu Lee and Charles were very proud, and now, Charles knew for certain that they had made the right move in coming to Lexington. Charles recognized that his wonderful wife, the love of his life, once again, had chosen the right path for all of them.

Lulu Lee initiated a very tight rein around Idalynn and Idalynn knew it was in her best interest to conform to it. Beginning a new phase in her life, Idalynn enrolled at the University of Kentucky in Lexington. Although she had the emotional capabilities of a young child, because of her intellect, she was able to assume the outward appearance of an adult. She was charming, witty, and could pretend to like the people that she needed, in order to succeed in school, as well as socially on campus. She had capabilities of masterminding the illusion that she was always right. In reality, she possessed the same characteristics of her father's in the business world. Idalynn was indeed a unique young lady.

Earning her Associate Degree in Teaching at the University, Idalynn attained her goal of becoming a kindergarten teacher. She was a delight, when it came to playing games or creating treasure hunts for the children and possessed an amazing ability in telling nursery rhymes and fairy tales. Re-enacting some of the stories' characters, Idalynn was able to stretch the imaginations of the children and the children blossomed under her care. Idalynn most assuredly had the love of all of the children and most importantly, the admiration of their parents.

Although Idalynn kept a certain facade about her, never allowing the real Idalynn to come forth, there did appear to be a change in her demeanor. She possessed a quiet softness about her. She surrounded herself with people who offered her friendship and warmth, and she was immensely popular with her crowd. Idalynn was happy and full of life. It seemed unthinkable that she was ever that young "Flapper girl" in Evansville, but only time would tell.

Idalynn was courted by many of the eligible bachelors of Lexington's most prominent families. Lulu Lee and Charles were very pleased with all the attention that the young professional men were affording Idalynn, but secretly wished that she would choose one man with whom to settle down. Idalynn seemed to enjoy falling in and out of love on a regular basis.

Several things that Idalynn's suitors had in common were they were reasonably handsome, had impeccable backgrounds, were sons of families from high society and most importantly, they had the means to support a wife in grand style. However, Idalynn never seemed to be fully enchanted by any of them. One by one, the young men, tired of being just one of many, vanished from the scene. They would eventually choose other young ladies as wives.

One evening at a friend's party, Idalynn met a young doctor, Roger Edmonds, who appeared instantly enamored with her. The attraction was mutual. Each appeared in awe of the other, he by her loveliness, she by his position and lifestyle.

After a very short courting time, Roger asked Idalynn for her hand in marriage, and Idalynn accepted his proposal—because, as she had told her friends, "She was passionately in love with him!"

When Roger approached Lulu Lee and Charles at their home to discuss his marriage proposal to their daughter, Lulu Lee was silently abashed. She could not understand how Idalynn could be planning such a giant step in her life, without their ever having met this gentleman or even ever having heard his name mentioned. Lulu Lee was exceptionally worried as Idalynn's past history showed; she at times had difficulty separating fantasy from reality. She was immature, and from past lifetime situations, unable to handle most emotional experiences.

In spite of her soul-searching thoughts, Lulu Lee reached out to Roger and hugged him. Charles shook Roger's hand and said, "I couldn't have chosen better, myself!"

After Roger's departure, Lulu Lee took Charles' hand and said, "Oh, Charles, what has she gone and done. I am so worried over this situation."

Charles insisted to his wife, "Lulu Lee, allow the engagement time to play out! Idalynn is almost twenty-five years old. We must loosen the reins and if necessary, let her fail and pick herself up! Only time would tell whether this engagement should move toward a wedding."

With Idalynn's ability to bend reality, while she was convincing others of her "match made in heaven" with Dr. Edmonds, Idalynn began to believe it herself. With Lulu Lee and Charles entering into her dreams, an elaborate engagement party was given for the couple by Idalynn's parents. Most assuredly, the best of Lexington had been invited. Once again, Idalynn was in the society column, which described the lovely couple and the elaborate celebration.

It was December, 1924. The holiday season in Lexington was opened with The Lexington Holiday Charity Ball. The invitation read:

Mr. and Mrs. Charles R. Spencer

and Daughter

Idalynn

are cordially invited to attend

The Lexington Holiday Charity Ball

December 18, 1924

Being the daughter, of one of the benefactors, of this most prestigious ball, Idalynn was expected to be one of the dance hostesses to those men who wished to sign on her dance card. Her fiancé, Roger, fully understood "the pressure" Idalynn was under, and said she had his complete blessings to do so. Roger promised to attend the ball, if his hospital schedule permitted. She told him, "I will mourn your absence until you arrive."

Michael Brooks

Idalynn was absolutely hypnotic! When she walked into the ballroom with her parents, her gown spoke to who she was. Wearing a floor length and flattering, red ball gown, she had the attention of all in the room. Her diminutive stature, along with her elegance and gracefulness on the dance floor, continued to create a flutter of conversation among most of the guests.

It was while she was dancing with one of the gentlemen whose name was on her dance card, that she looked up, and caught the glance of a tall and very handsome gentleman. She was later to learn his name was Michael Brooks.

Michael Brooks was a big man, in every sense of the word. Standing six feet tall, he possessed a shy smile that was much like that of a sunset: once shown, it became suddenly magnificent! It was this smile, along with his piercing green eyes with a subtle gaze that encouraged Idalynn to smile, coquettishly, in return. Michael gently nodded in her direction.

At the conclusion of the dance, Idalynn's dance partner escorted her off the floor to rejoin her friends. Michael Brooks was waiting there. Michael casually walked over to Idalynn and smiled as he introduced himself to her. "Good evening. Permit me to introduce myself. I'm Michael

Brooks. Perhaps is there room on your dance card for the two of us to enjoy a dance?"

Idalynn was at a loss for words, yet she could not help but be aware of the manner of this imposing man and how he looked at her. There was a sense of wonder, along with a beguiling strangeness and sense of intrigue that came over Idalynn. This was truly a moment she wanted to remember forever.

Finally, Idalynn smiled and said, "Well hello! I'm Idalynn Spencer.

"So I'm told. So I'm told," responded Michael.

Idalynn and Michael glided around the dance floor, lost within one another's presence. No one else around them seemed to matter. By the end of the dance, along with a few stolen moments of sharing conversation, Idalynn found herself mesmerized by this charming man. Michael thought Idalynn to be exquisite: he thought to himself that she was more beautiful than any other woman he had known.

When Michael suggested that they continue their en-counter over a glass of punch, as much as Idalynn wanted to do so, she declined. Roger had just entered the room and was approaching in her direction. Michael picked up on Idalynn's nervousness. "Perhaps we could meet again sometime?" Michael asked. Idalynn replied, "Yes! I would like that! Perhaps we could talk later." She was quick to say, "For the moment, will you not mention this to anyone?"

Michael said, "I'll find you." As he casually walked away, Roger walked up to Idalynn and kissed her on the cheek. Roger's greeting did not go unnoticed by Michael.

That evening, after Roger had taken her home and said good night, Idalynn rushed to her parents' room and said, "Oh, Mama! Oh, Daddy! This evening, I have met the man of my dreams!" Lulu Lee glanced at Charles. She was speechless. Charles was in shock! Idalynn spoke excitedly to both of her parents about Michael Brooks, as she told them of all the details of their chance encounter.

Lulu Lee asked, "Who is this Michael Brooks? Where is he from? What does he do for a living? I certainly didn't notice him at the ball!"

"Mama, all I know about him is he seems incredibly intelligent and he is from West Virginia and works for the government. I've agreed to see him again—that is if he ever calls. I didn't tell him where I lived or anything. He just said he would find me."

This was too much for Charles. "It all sounds so ominous!" Charles said. "Idalynn, for all you know he is a gangster! The fact that he works for the government means nothing! He could be a mailman or work in a federal penitentiary! Are you going to risk your engagement to this young nice doctor for some stranger, that by chance, came waltzing into your life?"

There was not much else Idalynn cared to say, but "Maybe. Only time will tell!" Then Idalynn twirled out of the room as though she were on cloud nine. In so many words, she let her parents know that she was going to do whatever she pleased. She was not interested in their opinions.

When they were alone, Charles commented to Lulu Lee, "Idalynn is so misguided! She does not think realistically." But Charles also knew that they were responsible for her being unpredictable and very spoiled. Regardless, Charles said, "I'm not going to just stand by and watch this child destroy her life over some man that she thinks is incredibly intelligent. It took all these years before she finally settled on one man, Dr. Edmonds and now this! I am immediately going to have an investigation of who ever this Michael Brooks is!" One thing that lay heavily on Charles' mind was whether or not Idalynn would resent them for being so protective, should she find out that he was having Michael investigated.

While Charles Spencer was ranting, Lulu Lee could only think to herself that Idalynn had not even mentioned Roger Edmonds being present at the ball. Lulu Lee knew that her daughter would not have dared to tell Roger of her interesting encounter with Michael Brooks. Of course, Lulu Lee, nor Charles were about to mention it.

———

True to his word, Michael called Idalynn the very next day. Idalynn could not help but be thrilled beyond words, and it showed in her voice to him. Michael said, "I have so little time to spend here in Lexington, before I must leave. May I call upon you this evening?"

Idalynn was hesitant, but overjoyed at the same time. She responded, "That would be so nice. May I tell you where I live?"

Michael chuckled and said, "I know where you live. That's my business. But tell me, will this be a problem for you?" Idalynn assured him that it would not, and a time was set.

Idalynn hung up the phone and rushed to tell her mother. "It's like Daddy always said, punctuality and consideration go hand in hand. You can't say he isn't punctual or considerate! He said he would call, and he did!"

When Lulu Lee called Charles at the office to prepare him for meeting Michael Brooks, Charles informed Lulu Lee that one of his contacts had just returned his call regarding Michael. Charles continued, "Lulu Lee, Michael is a Treasury Agent for the United States Government, a T-Man traveling and making inspections and investigations for the Internal Revenue Service Alcohol Division. The report also said that Michael was originally from a Wisconsin town, not far from Chicago."

Charles went on to tell Lulu Lee, "Michael Brooks is the Executive Head in the Federal Prohibition Department at

Charleston, West Virginia, and that he is also holding positions in Huntington, Parkersburg, and Wheeling. The report says Michael was regarded as the most efficient and competent Treasury Agent in the Federal Prohibition Department in the state of West Virginia. The report also stated that he was highly honored and a highly esteemed gentleman."

Now Charles understood why Michael, by nature of his career, was such a private man. Charles and Lulu Lee were relieved and smiled.

———

As fate would allow, Roger Edmonds called that afternoon to apologize to Idalynn for needing to cancel some of their immediate holiday plans, as he had been requested by his chief surgeon to attend a medical convention in Louisville for the next few days. He promised to call her every evening while he was away.

That evening when Michael arrived at the Spencer home, Charles was reading in the living room. Lulu Lee was the one to greet him at the door. Upon hearing Michael's voice, Charles jumped up to meet this man that his daughter had found to be so charming.

Michael introduced himself to Charles and Lulu Lee. Taking off his hat, Michael said, "Good evening, Mrs. Spencer. Good evening to you, sir. Permit me to introduce myself. I'm Michael Brooks. I'm from Charleston, West Virginia."

Charles responded, "Good evening, Michael. How nice to meet you. What brings you to Lexington, all the way from West Virginia?" Not acknowledging that he knew anything about Michael, Charles prompted Michael into telling them of his reason for being at the Lexington Charity Ball.

Michael smiled and in a slow and easy manner said, "Mr. Spencer, I was honored with an invitation from your Mayor, Mr. Bishop. I had previously met him at Governor Howard Gore's home in Charleston." Charles caught his wife's glance and nod of approval.

Idalynn quickly interjected, "Mother, Dad, perhaps we could all sit down sometime soon and talk much more, but for now, do you mind if Michael and I just dash. We don't want dinner to be too late." In essence, Idalynn did not want to be in the house should Roger call from Louisville.

The Spencer's devotion to their daughter made them feel guilty for occupying so much of the young couple's time. Laughing, they said, "You are absolutely correct, Idalynn. We will look forward to another time to hold this enlightening conversation."

Michael assisted Idalynn with her coat, as they bid goodbye. Lulu Lee and Charles were both in agreement that this imposing young man had made a very nice impression. Now they only wondered how this scene would play out! They wondered about Roger. What was Idalynn thinking?

Returning home that evening, Idalynn ran upstairs to her parents' bedroom and was met by her awaiting parents. Lulu Lee asked, "How was your evening, dear?"

Idalynn responded, "Oh Mother, Daddy, I have had the most unforgettable evening and I am desperately in love!" Lulu Lee and Charles gasped! After all this was only the second time that their daughter had been in his company.

Not sharing any more details about her evening with Michael, Idalynn left her parents' room to go to her own room to just think and relive the extraordinary evening that she had just had. Idalynn envisioned that she was embarking upon a wonderful romance—again. Idalynn also did not show any interest when her mother had told her that Roger had indeed called.

———————

With the Christmas holidays ahead, there were festivities abounding, and Idalynn wanted to be free to share them with Michael, whenever he could be in town. She had to think about how all this could be arranged. For the moment, Idalynn didn't think that she wanted to lose Roger, but she also knew that she wanted to be with Michael... maybe with Roger's busy schedule at the hospital, he wouldn't be aware—She knew she would need her parents to assist her in this deception. She knew that she could count on her father, but knew all too well that her mother would be most upset with her.

———————————

Within a short time, Idalynn and Michael seemed to be inseparably entwined. There was no pressure between the two of them; neither asked for commitment from the other. Idalynn's happiness was in dreaming of what the future might hold.

Idalynn finally decided to break her engagement to Roger. She knew she would need to return her engagement ring to him. She also knew it had to be done with dignity. Idalynn implored her father to speak with Roger for her. In that fashion, she would not have to face any unpleasant situation, and that would make it much easier on her! She begged her father to accept this duty for her.

With unwavering devotion to his daughter, Charles made an appointment to meet with Roger, to deliver Idalynn's message and engagement ring. Charles, trying to convince Roger that Idalynn and he were not suited for each other, as they were remarkably different personalities, Charles, asked Roger to let the healing process begin.

Devouring every word that Mr. Spencer said, Roger responded, "I didn't see this coming. I was never aware that Idalynn and I had any problems between us. She had me completely convinced that our romance was a match made in Heaven. We shared such wonderful times. I am devastated!" In silence, he walked out of Mr. Spencer's office, thinking that he had only wanted a few minutes alone with Idalynn, but Idalynn would not even take his calls. She thought it unladylike to face controversy. Roger walked away and out of Idalynn's life forever.

Idalynn's actions were typical of her past behaviors. She always did things her way—regardless of consequences. Charles Spencer had created what Idalynn was; as a result, Idalynn would one day pay an even greater price for her erratic decisions in her life.

———————————

Michael came to Lexington from Charleston, whenever time and work permitted. Idalynn was attracted to Michael's magnetic image, while Michael felt an aura of mystery between them. Their romance was a combined adventure for both of them, and it was working.

Decisions

The following March, 1925, Michael invited Idalynn and her parents to be his guests at Governor Howard Gore's Inaugural Ceremonies and Ball in Charleston.

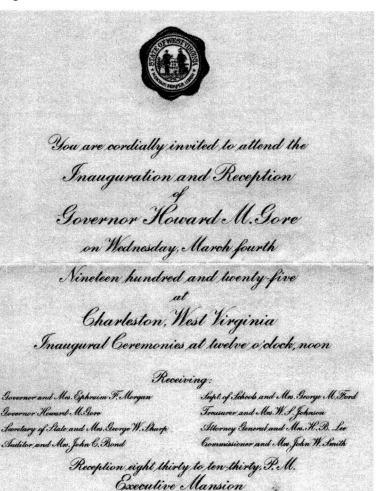

You are cordially invited to attend the

Inauguration and Reception

of

Governor Howard M. Gore

on Wednesday, March fourth

Nineteen hundred and twenty-five

at

Charleston, West Virginia

Inaugural Ceremonies at twelve o'clock, noon

Receiving:

Governor and Mrs. Ephraim F. Morgan   Supt. of Schools and Mrs. George M. Ford
Governor Howard M. Gore   Treasurer and Mrs. W. S. Johnson
Secretary of State and Mrs. George W. Sharp   Attorney General and Mrs. H. B. Lee
Auditor and Mrs. John C. Bond   Commissioner and Mrs. John W. Smith

Reception eight thirty to ten thirty, P. M.

Executive Mansion

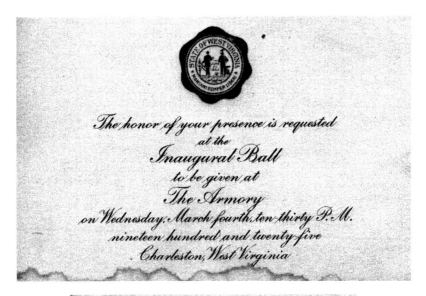

*The honor of your presence is requested
at the
Inaugural Ball
to be given at
The Armory
on Wednesday, March fourth, ten-thirty P.M.
nineteen hundred and twenty-five
Charleston, West Virginia*

*The Armory
Wednesday, March Fourth
Nineteen hundred and twenty-five
Charleston
West Virginia*

Idalynn and her parents, accepted graciously.

Word circulated at the ball that evening that Michael Brooks and Idalynn Spencer were one of the most attractive couples in attendance. It was written in the next day's social column;

"Spectacular would be an inadequate word to describe Idalynn Spencer from Lexington, Kentucky. They are definitely a couple to watch!"

———————

In the meantime, life was moving at a fast pace for the Spencers. The brothers made plans to expand their business to another meat packing plant—this time on the Leestown Pike.

Charles mentioned to Lulu Lee that he had a desire to independently open a creamery business. Lulu Lee was elated when Charles told her he was thinking about opening a cheese creamery in Horse Cave. Lulu Lee said, "Oh Charles, going into business back home has always been a dream of mine. I would be so pleased and proud to contribute to my community."

Charles had been made aware that there was a possible location on Water Street that he wanted to consider. Lulu Lee, of course, knew exactly where the location was and thought it would be perfect. In her mind, it was a spiritual connection to her mother. Lulu Lee also knew her father would not only be immensely proud, but pleased that she would be coming home.

She exclaimed, "Oh Charlie, I must call my father and tell him today."

Mr. Taylor was elated to hear of the exciting plans of a future creamery right there in Horse Cave. He excitedly told anyone who would listen. Unfortunately, before Lulu Lee and Charles could move forward with any of these plans, Lulu Lee's father suffered a stroke and died, shortly after she had visited Mulberry. Lulu Lee was especially thankful that Jennie and her husband had been with her father during his final years of his life.

Plans to open a creamery in Horse Cave were shelved for the present. Charles thought that perhaps being in Horse Cave developing the business would be too hard on Lulu Lee at this time. She was so overwhelmed just thinking about all of her memories of living there with her mother and father, both of whom were in the past. She just didn't want to think about a business in Horse Cave.

When Charles mentioned another location in Waynesboro, Tennessee to Lulu Lee, she agreed that he should move forward with his plans. His vision was to establish a creamery and a meat packing plant on the same site. Although his two brothers did not want to venture out of the Lexington area, they encouraged Charles to go forth alone with his plans.

With Charles' golden touch, the Waynesboro plant turned out to be an unparalleled success. But Charles did tell Lulu Lee that his priority to open a creamery in her hometown was still in the working stage.

In years to come, several other creameries would be established, as well as several Kentucky Cheese Stores throughout the states of Kentucky and Tennessee. Self- appointed, Charles would become the President of the Kentucky Dairy Association.

Michael Brooks needed to journey to Washington D. C. to appear before the Judiciary Committee of the U.S. House of Representatives. The Congressional Committee was conducting a hearing concerning prohibition enforcement. It was while Michael was in Washington that he was informed he was being transferred to Chicago, to become Superintendent of the U.S. Warehouse of Federal Prohibition Department.

Knowing he would be leaving the area in which Idalynn lived, Michael wrote to her to ask her for her hand in marriage. He told Idalynn of his plans to work in the Prohibition Department, as well as to enter the University of Chicago Law School at night to complete his law degree.

Idalynn was ecstatic! She rushed to tell her mother of Michael's proposal. "Oh, Mother, I'm so happy! I've accepted Michael's proposal to marry him! He's all that I've ever wanted. He's so wonderful! He's sweet and shy and he has gorgeous eyes! He's tall and so very handsome, and Mother, he makes me laugh! I must wire Michael immediately, telling him, ABSOLUTELY!"

Michael was so pleased and very proud to receive Idalynn's wire that read, "I shall go wherever you go!" Her parents, Lulu Lee and Charles, although showing happiness on their faces, could not help but be worried if this was the right path for their daughter to be going down.

But Idalynn's protective life, that she had always led, deflective of any responsibility, and with total love and support of her family, was to pay a heavy price. She had never before been without her family. Deep within herself, Idalynn, had an air of hesitancy, along with a sense of what she was about to lose. Idalynn asked herself repeatedly, "Why had I promised him to go wherever he goes?"

Idalynn began to feel uncertain, regarding this new phase of her life to come, with a new husband who would be taking her to a new life in a Northern city. In short, Idalynn looked back on a life that she was leaving behind, and began to rethink this bold step that she was about to take. Along with feelings of sadness, she harbored feelings of resentment toward Michael—the man, "that made her laugh."

On an impulse, or perhaps out of desperation, Idalynn begged her father to offer Michael an executive position, with a high dollar income, in Spencer Brothers, Inc. or perhaps the Kentucky Cheese Company. She wanted Michael to establish himself in Lexington and grow to love her city as much as she did.

Not wanting to lose his daughter to another part of the country, but more importantly, never denying his daughter any wish, Charles invited Michael to his office, during any time that he would be in town. It seemed almost too recent that he had invited Roger Edmonds to discuss his daughter's romantic illusions.

Michael, believing that this meeting was more than likely the usual prenuptial discussion of fatherly concerns for his daughter, went directly to Mr. Spencer's office at his first opportunity. Charles was waiting for Michael at his office door.

Greeting Michael enthusiastically, Charles put his arm over Michael's shoulders and suggested they take a tour of the plant. As they walked through the various divisions, Charles said, "Well, what do you think about all this?" Michael commented, "The meat packing business is certainly very interesting."

Charles asked Michael, "What do you know about meats?"

Michael answered, "Not very much I'm afraid, in spite of being raised on a farm."

"Well, do you think you could learn about sales?" asked Charles. "It's all about people skills, you know."

Before Michael could assimilate what Charles was proposing, Charles said, "I have an idea...let's have a game of poker."

Michael replied, "I have never played poker in my life."

Charles said, "I can teach you." Having said that, Charles brought out a deck of cards and started to explain the rudiments of the game. Out of courtesy and respect, Michael listened.

Charles said, "Young man, playing poker is educational! It makes a person mentally sharp. He has to concentrate and to know every card that has been played. One has to be alert and judge his opponent's hand. He has to be quick and mentally shrewd. I would say that once you are a good poker player, you would also be a good businessman; and Michael, I'd be proud to have my son-in-law, working along side of me, on my team!"

Michael hesitated for a moment and then countered, "I'm overwhelmed that you have offered me a position with Spencer Brothers, and I thank you for that, but I'm afraid the selling game is not for me. My interests lie with the government. I plan to study Law."

The scene just played out, was exactly the scene that had been played between Charles and his future father-in-law, Winston Taylor many years ago, when he wanted Charles to be on the plantation, and Charles wanted to be a salesman. Charles understood completely, and took the conversation no further.

At that moment, Idalynn walked into the office and took Michael's arm and smiled up at him. "Michael, darling, are you pleased with my father's offer?" she asked.

Michael put his arms around Idalynn and said, "Your father is a very generous man, and I am honored by his offer, but for now Idalynn, we need to think about our wedding plans and our own lives ahead of us, in Chicago."

Michael was not immediately aware of the look of disbelief that came over Idalynn's face. She was struggling to come to terms with her emotions, as well as trying to deal with the fact that there had been no acceptance from Michael of her father's generous offer of employment.

Idalynn questioned, "Michael, is there not a possibility that you could find fulfillment as an executive in Spencer Brothers Meat Packing Plant? Not only would we be home here in Lexington, we'd lead a life of privilege. My parents would see to it."

Idalynn looked to her father for assurance. She wanted him to jump into this discussion and say something. Charles gazed downward and offered no comment.

Knowing Michael was the obstinate part of the equation, Idalynn fled the office in tears—alone. Michael looked at Charles and said, "It seems that my wife-to-be, has an obsession about living in Lexington!" Now it was Charles thinking to himself, "Why would anyone want to leave Kentucky?"

Idalynn felt the pangs of desperation consuming her. She asked herself, why would Michael re-act so unkindly

toward not only her family, but to her? She was disappointed and saddened beyond words! In the meantime, Lulu Lee
and Charles realized that a formal announcement of their
daughter's impending wedding needed to be made.

———————

A wedding date of June twenty- first was set in Lexington.
The society columns read that "Mr. Brooks was most assuredly a man with great destiny, and that the Spencer/Brooks
wedding would be one of Lexington's social events of the
year."

Idalynn knew she would be entering an unfamiliar world,
being married to Michael. After thoroughly thinking of the
probability of a marriage, she realized that she had no desire to run a household. It was the antithesis of whatever
she wanted to be. Even menial tasks were more than she
chose to undertake. The extent of her cooking capabilities
was making fudge or white divinity candy. For that matter,
she had never styled her own auburn hair. Her clothes had
always been cared for, and laid out for her to wear.

From Michael's perspective, this marriage was to last a
lifetime; but Idalynn's parents, knowing their daughter's
mercurial romantic past, felt that Idalynn was more in love
with having a wedding than having a marriage. They feared
that this future marriage was already on shaky grounds.

Although Idalynn had eagerly accepted Michael's proposal, now going north to Chicago no longer seemed to her to be an exotic location. She felt entangled in a web. Idalynn silently harbored intense ill feelings toward Michael, feeling he wanted no part of her family or living in Lexington. The fact that it was his desire to become an attorney had no bearing on her and did not play into her scheme of things. Idalynn decided to tell her mother that she was planning to call off the wedding, as this romance no longer seemed to be as wonderful as seen through the eyes of others.

Thinking her mother would be immeasurably pleased, Idalynn approached her mother to tell her of her decision to cancel the wedding and remain in Lexington. Idalynn said, "Mama, after much deliberation, I have decided to call off my wedding to Michael. I have had second thoughts and know now that perhaps Roger would have been the better choice."

Idalynn was shocked, when her mother countered, "Idalynn, it would be very ill mannered on your part to do such a thing as to cancel your wedding to Michael. I absolutely forbid you to vacillate between Michael and Roger. I implore you to show ingrained grace, be a beautiful and elegant bride, and even more importantly, be a good wife to Michael."

Having just said that, Lulu Lee could not help but remember how she, too, had not wanted to leave her southern roots to go north, but out of her love for Charlie agreed to do so.

Lulu Lee admonished her daughter. "Idalynn, you are no longer a child. You need to trust in your choice that you have made to marry Michael." Lulu Lee continued, "You'll see everything will be fine." Inwardly, Lulu Lee was more than concerned. She wished now that she had permitted Idalynn to grow emotionally. She knew she had been derelict in this manner.

A flood of tears streamed down Idalynn's face. She felt that she was being devoured and being forced to proceed with these wedding plans. This proposed wedding, factoring in all the unknowns, was simply too much for her to handle. She felt cornered and even trapped!

The sole factor was, Idalynn dreaded leaving her life in Lexington. She asked herself, "What about my English Bulldog, Pat Bailey? I simply can't leave him. I also know I can't take him with me. I am not even certain just where I will be living." Idalynn thought to herself that she had a lifestyle that she loved, and a teaching career that she had worked hard to create. Now she had reached the realization that what had played out in the previous months was a sudden romance and the enormity of a life ahead with Michael frightened her. Nevertheless, her parents went on with wedding plans.

Mr. and Mrs. Charles R. Spencer

Announce the betrothal of their daughter

Idalynn

To

Mr. Michael A. Brooks

On the twenty-first of June

Nineteen hundred and twenty-seven

It was Idalynn's wedding day and Charles knew that he was relinquishing his only daughter, his only child, to a man who would take her north. He knew he had to resign himself to the fact that he might not see her very often in the future. He would miss seeing Idalynn running in and out of the house, hearing her laughter, as well as their father and daughter talks. The somber look on his face gave way to the fact that although he too wished that all of this would just disappear, he knew he had to accept what was about to take place.

True to her Kentucky roots, the bride, carrying a mixed bouquet of orange blossoms and baby's breath, was a lovely vision in a robe de style gown of white Elizabethan crepe, trimmed with rhinestones and exquisite lace. In Idalynn's hair, was a band of orange blossoms and rhinestones.

Descending the staircase that had been lushly decorated with orange blossoms, she was met by her father at the bottom of the stairs to be escorted to the living room fireplace where the ceremony was about to take place. Charles, gazing at Idalynn, through his own misty eyes, noticed that she appeared to be in a trance.

Charles tried his best to smile at his daughter. She in turn tried her best to feign happiness on this day of uncertainty. While Michael and the wedding party and guests were waiting, Charles whispered to his daughter, "Remember, you never tell everything about yourself." Idalynn winked at her father. Idalynn was twenty-eight years old. Idalynn had told Michael she was twenty-three.

Upon reaching the fireplace, Michael took Idalynn's arm in his. Known only to a few, there was a dichotomy existing between the families of the bride and groom. Michael's parents were farmers, owning a large farm in Wisconsin. They were elated that their son was finally coming closer to home with a lovely bride—a daughter that they could teach many aspects of cooking and canning; and if need be some of the rudiments of farming itself. They were thrilled that she would be a part of their Wisconsin family.

Conversely, Idalynn's parents could only focus on Idalynn's moving far away from them and not so much would be gaining a son, but more importantly, they would be losing their daughter.

While all the guests enjoyed the beautiful day, Idalynn could only wish that all this was a bad dream. She questioned to herself, "How did fate lead me to this point?" She feared what tomorrow might hold!

Not known to anyone, this marriage of elegance, that society had written was "a romance comparable to none," would bring a life of tragedy, not only to the newlyweds, but to those who loved her the most.

A Different World

For a short time, Idalynn tried her best to accept her new life in Chicago as Michael's wife. They settled into a very lovely, downtown apartment, paying a rental fee of almost three hundred dollars—an extraordinary amount for the late 1920's. It was fun for her to select new furniture, lamps, and accessories. Idalynn kept herself busy looking through decorating magazines in order that she might emulate the latest decorating ideas. But mostly, Idalynn, not realizing it, was emulating the furnishings of the home she had just left back in Lexington—Mulberry.

Michael accepted the fact that he and Idalynn were from two different worlds. Not forgetting that Idalynn came from a life of opulence and culture, and by virtue of how she was raised was helpless when it came to domesticities. Michael said, "Idalynn, don't worry about anything. We will learn together as we go."

Idalynn assured Michael that housekeeping was fun. She said, "I'm going to do my best. It can't be that difficult!" However, the first opportunity Idalynn had, she called her mother to tell her how overwhelmed she was—to the point of a breakdown.

"Mama, I am so distraught. I have tried so hard to create a lovely home, clean, cook meals, and entertain Michael's friends and I just can't do it. I am so tired and I am so tired of crying over missing you and Daddy. Help me! What am I going to do?"

Her pleas to her mother only reminded Idalynn more of the days when she had the complete attention and devotion of her parents. Always having so many friends, now even friendships seemed to elude her. Idalynn just couldn't seem to open her heart to a new life up north—away from Mulberry. She asked her mother to intercede for her with her father, to see if he would send her money to employ a housekeeper, as well as a cook.

Of course Charles was only too happy to answer her request. Idalynn's happiness was his first priority in life.

With the employment of household help, Idalynn told Michael, "Being a homemaker is a pleasure for me. It is so much fun!" Of course, Idalynn always made certain that her hired help was gone, long before Michael returned from work. Her father's adage, "Never tell everything about yourself!" was foremost in her mind.

Working during the daytime for the Justice Department and attending law school during the evenings occupied all of Michael's time. Idalynn found herself not only alone, but lonely. This life of being married was not which she had envisioned. She was disillusioned, unhappy and bored with her life in Chicago. Consequently, Idalynn spent a good portion of her time thinking about, and missing, the previous life she had once lived.

The harsh reality of living in Chicago, far away from her family and with no friends to share her life, was beginning to affect her in many ways. Not only was it a very warm summer in Chicago, even the smell of the fumes of buses moving slowly in traffic on the street made her ill. Idalynn could not agree less when she read that the Chicago Chamber of Commerce prided itself in saying, "Chicago Is Where It all Happens!"

It was a simple fact in Idalynn's mind that it was just too difficult to endure this life with Michael. Idalynn regretted the choice she had made to leave her past behind. It was imperative for her to be able to persuade Michael that after he graduated from law school, they should return to Lexington to continue their lives.

Idalynn had already discussed with her father the possibility of Michael being retained as an attorney for Spencer Brothers. Charles assured Idalynn that there would always be a place for Michael in the company. With an offer such as this from her father, Idalynn felt that there would also be a guarantee of happiness. Idalynn planned to propose the idea to Michael. She held the thought that if Michael turned down the idea of moving back to Lexington, she would move back alone.

Michael graduated from the University of Chicago Law School, and with his Doctoral Thesis on Radio Law was offered the position of Associate Dean of the Chicago Law School. While Michael was flattered by this offer and accepted, Idalynn was downtrodden. Her dream to return to her home in Lexington, was shattered.

Over several months time, Michael's life in Chicago was filled with success and exciting challenges. Endorsed by ministers of foreign countries, several United States Senators, as well as John W. Davis, former ambassador to England, President Calvin Coolidge offered Michael a diplomatic post in the American Foreign Service at the American Legation in Managua, Nicaragua.

Michael was tempted to accept this offer, as he had thoughts of possibly tossing his own hat into the political ring one day. He was eager to tell Idalynn of this recognition from the President of the United States, but he knew it had to be mentioned in a proper manner, at the proper time.

It was early December. Michael asked Idalynn "What do you think about driving back to Lexington for the holidays?" Idalynn was overjoyed just thinking about it. Idalynn exclaimed, "Michael! That would be the best Christmas present ever!"

Michael responded, "Then, Let's do it! Call your parents and tell them, we're coming home!"

Idalynn rushed to the telephone. Upon placing the call, her father answered. Hearing her father's voice, Idalynn said, "Oh Daddy, We're coming home for the holidays! It will be the school holidays at the University, and we can have a whole three weeks to be together. Quick! Put Mama on the phone!"

Charles was as excited as Idalynn. He said, "Idalynn, this will be a wonderful time for all of us! There are galas and of course, the Charity Ball to attend. Bring something striking to wear! Don't forget Michael's tuxedo! Here's your mother!"

"Mama. I'll be home soon. It'll be so wonderful to see you both again!" exclaimed Idalynn. "Be sure to tell Pat Bailey, I'm coming home!"

Walking away from the telephone, Idalynn couldn't keep her mind on anything except the trip back home to Lexington. In just a few days, she and Michael would be enjoying the holidays with her parents. There would also be so many friends to see and places to go. It was going to be such a festive time!

Arriving home In Lexington, her dog, Pat Bailey, barked, jumped and spun in circles over his excitement in greeting her. Idalynn went directly to her room to place her luggage, as well as to absorb being in the place she loved best—her room. It was still the same. She could still smell the aroma of her own favorite perfume that she had always worn. It was in this room that she remembered laughing with her girl friends about their various dates. It was also in this room that she donned her first formal prom dress and admired herself in the long petticoat mirror—the same mirror that Grandmother Angelines had gazed upon herself on the day of Lulu Lee and Charles' wedding. Idalynn thought to herself that so much history had played out in front of this mirror.

Idalynn looked over at her old phonograph machine and remembered how she played and danced to the music and songs of Rudy Vallee. It was such a wonderful feeling, just recalling the memories of so many good times. Her eyes started to brim with tears. "I'm home," Idalynn thought." I'm home and I don't ever want to leave!" Of course that was unrealistic thinking; but that was exactly what she was thinking.

It was while dining with the Spencers that evening, Michael proudly mentioned to all, the offer of a Nicaraguan diplomatic post that had been offered to him by the President of the United States.

Charles was astounded! "My word, Michael! That is a real feather in our hats," he said.

Lulu Lee said, "Oh my, Michael! Is that something that you would really like to do? Where is Nicaragua?"

Idalynn was wide-eyed, and trying to absorb as much as she could understand. Michael, noticing her anguish, and trying to defuse the situation that he thought was about to happen said, "It is only a two-year assignment and the increase in pay will be great! I'm rather excited about accepting this offer and look forward to the opportunity."

Idalynn threw her napkin down on the table, looked directly at Michael and said, "Why didn't you mention this to me before? Did you think breaking it to me in front of my parents would make it acceptable to me? Michael, this is so cruel of you! I absolutely will have no part of it! Wherever this place is, you will go to it alone, and believe me, you will suffer the consequences!" And Idalynn left the table in tears, fleeing to her room.

Idalynn was angry with Michael for the manner in which he had shocked her with his plans to go to Nicaragua. Idalynn felt the omission of his not telling her about all of this was the same as a lie. The business of money was distasteful to her. The fact that he would jeopardize her happiness only made her angrier. She was most displeased with his being offered an ambassadorship. In reality, she was questioning the status of her marriage. This was the second time during her life with Michael that he had brought much emotional pain to her.

She remembered when Michael would not consider a position that her father had offered to him before they were married—a position that held great promise for him. Instead, he chose to take her to another part of the country. Now, this time, this surprise announcement that had been sprung on her would take her to another part of the world!

Inwardly, she wondered if perhaps this was the excuse that she should use to stay in Lexington?

Downstairs, Michael, still sitting at the table, with the Spencers was speechless. No one said a word. The tone had obviously been set for the evening. He excused himself and went directly to Idalynn. He soon realized that the tone had been set for the entire holidays!

Perhaps, lacking the confidence to be far, far away from her family in Lexington, Idalynn begged Michael to refuse this diplomatic post. She didn't care what others would say about her refusal to be any part of a life in a foreign country. Cloaked by Idalynn's sadness and feelings, upon returning to Chicago the politically ambitious Michael reluctantly turned down the offer of a United States Ambassadorship.

Michael continued his work at the University, trying not to give in to his feelings that he had truly missed a once-in-a-lifetime opportunity. He was restless and seemed remarkably different. He worked late hours at the University and when he was home, his conversations with Idalynn seemed stoic. Without question, Michael's demeanor had changed.

—————————

Because of so much respect for Michael's impeccable reputation and past record, a second offer of Diplomatic International Service as a clerk in the Legation of Managua, was offered to him from the Secretary of State in Washington, during the following year.

Again, with Idalynn's adamant refusal to be any part of his life if he chose this assignment, Michael once more, stepped back from the offer. With this second refusal, any possibility of a career in politics for Michael came to an end. Without question, there was enormous pressure building between the young couple.

Michael no longer found fulfillment in his work at the University. He was disconcerted and possessed an unwavering compulsion to return to his previous life with the government. Fearing that choice of a career, Idalynn repeatedly asked him to reconsider his thoughts about resigning from the law school. Ambivalent himself of what path he should pursue, Michael wanted to discuss his thoughts with his father-in-law.

Calling Charles, he said, "Father Spencer, help me sort out my thoughts, regarding what would be best for Idalynn and myself. My work at the law school is certainly a result of my love for the law, but in saying that, I believe my life's passion to be not instructing about the law, but enforcing the law. I was never happier in my work than when I was a government agent in the Prohibition Department. I know if I go with government law enforcement, I will be able to secure a position right here in Chicago. It would not require a move."

Charles' heart was heavy. He knew by encouraging Michael in what would make him the happiest he in effect, was betraying his daughter. Finally, Charles said, "Michael, we met and accepted you as a "T-man." I encourage you to return to that very successful time of your life."

Feeling that he must do what would ultimately be best for both of them, Michael offered his resignation to the University of Chicago Law School. Idalynn was incensed. She did not feel that this was best for her! Now, Idalynn was facing her first real life's challenge.

The Untouchables

Having previously spent twelve years with the Treasury Department, Michael returned to life as a "T-Man" in the Justice Department—the chief investigators of Prohibition in Chicago. Much to Idalynn's distain, Michael joined forces with the legendary crime fighter, Eliot Ness, who had been placed in charge of Prohibition by J. Edgar Hoover, head of the Federal Bureau of Investigation, because of this relationship they became life long friends. Pursuit of gangster, Al Capone, was their mission. Now for certain, Idalynn was living in a state of fear, worrying not only about Michael, but herself as well.

Accompanying Eliot Ness, Michael raided warehouses and arrested beer runners, as well as illegal distillers of bathtubgin. Gangster Al Capone boasted that he knew that some "G Men" (government men) could be "bought off." Eliot Ness funneled words back to Capone that it wasn't to be the case with him.

With Michael as his assistant, Eliot Ness formed an elite group of nine men and named them, "The Untouchables"— those who couldn't be bought or frightened away. Having received many tips of gangster rendezvous, not once revealing his sources, Michael even had the faith of the underworld. He was an efficient and highly regarded enforcement agent.

On several occasions, Mr. Ness came to the Brooks' apartment to discuss various modes of operation. One evening, Idalynn became concerned while listening to comments made by Ness, to Michael, of a `job well done' regarding an incident involving machine guns at a gangsters' roadblock. Michael had narrowly escaped death by making a U-turn with his car in the middle of the road, and outrunning the gangsters who were chasing him, under a hail of bullets.

During another meeting at their home, Idalynn listened to Mr. Ness offer Michael a commendation regarding Michael's most recent brush with death. He had been covering a farmhouse that was suspected of being a still for moonshine. Michael had been hiding in the tall brush, outside of the farmhouse, and needed to return to his car, which was parked down the road, to talk on his two-way radio. While he was at his car, he heard a loud explosion, and looked up to see the farm home on fire. Running back toward the house, Michael saw the place where he had been hiding, covered with the burning roof of the house. Had he not moved from that point earlier, he would most assuredly been killed.

Upon hearing this last saga, Idalynn paled. Michael noticed the look on Idalynn's face and knew he had a lot of explaining to do to her. He also knew he had a lot of downplaying to do about his career. Idalynn was furious that Michael held what she called "little regard" for his own self, or for the possibility of leaving her a widow—a title that repulsed her.

Michael, like most "T-Men," was a quiet man who blended into society and never talked about details of any dangerous assignments. He did not mention to Idalynn, that he would be with another government man, Melvin Purvis, when, the plan was to surround the Biograph Movie Theatre in downtown Chicago to capture John Dillinger.

When it was over, Michael asserted to Idalynn that he had not fired his gun at Mr. Dillinger during this ambush. This assertion was of little comfort, if any to Idalynn.

With Michael leading a life of undercover in the crime world, there were times when he would leave their home in the morning, and not return for several days. Such was the nature of his job. Unbeknownst to Idalynn whether he was dead or alive, she made it clear to Michael that this lifestyle was unacceptable to her and had to cease! Her nervous tensions along with this manner of living, only added strong discord to their marriage.

On one occasion, Michael worked undercover for several weeks with a gang of criminals, until he had enough evidence on them for a conviction. The newspaper headline said of Michael, "He Keeps a Secret." It had also been a secret to his wife!

HE KEEPS A SECRET

One evening, Idalynn and Michael went out for an evening of dancing at the Bal Tabarin Cafe, in the Sherman Hotel. Michael had made reservations, under an alias name of W. T. Burton. Only when they arrived at the café, and Michael gave the name, "Burton" at the reservation desk, was Idalynn made aware that this was not to be just a social evening of dance. She became very angry, when Michael told her, that a police raid was to take place that evening at that particular club.

The moment arrived! The raid started! Someone threw a tear gas bomb! Michael recognized the odor of the gas bomb immediately and rushed to get Idalynn out of the back entrance of the café. With her blue eyes tearing, she was not able to find one of her shoes that she had removed under the table. She was incensed with Michael for putting her in harm's way. And, she was very angry that she had lost a shoe, belonging to a favorite pair.

A Baby on the Way

Back in Lexington, Lulu Lee, still trying to fill the void of Idalynn's presence no longer in the house, reached a decision to devote herself to young girls from correctional institutions that needed personal guidance in their lives. Lulu Lee felt these girls, about to become young ladies, needed polishing and culture. Only then could they attain suitable positions in life. Permitting some of the girls to live in her home, the girls assisted Lulu Lee with domestic chores, until they found professional positions. Lulu Lee looked upon this as her charity to society.

It was during this time in Lulu Lee's life that Idalynn called home to tell her parents that they would soon become grandparents. "This is such wonderful news, Idalynn" said Lulu Lee. "Charles! Quickly! Come to the phone!" Lulu Lee and Charles could only think that now, they would have the opportunity to cuddle another baby that would almost be their very own. They were both excited and enjoyed much "happy talk" with one another.

Over the months, Idalynn wrote many letters to her mother telling her the latest news regarding the expected baby, as well as asking her for advice—whether it was about baby clothes or baby furniture needed.

One troublesome vein of thought always persisted in Idalynn's letters to Lulu Lee. Idalynn wrote, "Mama, I have mixed emotions about having this baby. Having a baby makes me instinctively vulnerable, as I feel that I am laying deeper roots here in Chicago, nearer to Michael's parents, rather than to you and Dad. Mama, I want you to know that I have no intentions of raising my child in Chicago!"

It was November. The first grandchild, a baby girl, was born at home and welcomed, with much love. Lulu Lee was overjoyed when she was told that the baby was her namesake but would be called Lee. It was only at this time did the memories of Idalynn's birth, also born at home in November, with both grandmothers rushing to meet their namesake, help Lulu Lee understand how each must have felt. Now, she too, was preparing to rush to Idalynn's side, to meet and hold her first grandchild—and namesake!

Charles assisted Lulu Lee in boarding her train for Chicago to meet their precious grandchild. Charles stated, "I wish that I could be going as well." Lulu Lee promised him, that she would call frequently, to give him updates of the brand new addition to the family. With the train's last call for boarding, Lulu Lee said, "Now promise me Charles that you will not overwork and you will take care of yourself. Bye, Bye dear. I love you!"

Dorothy, one of Lulu Lee's young trainees, was left in charge of the household and preparing meals for Charles while Lulu Lee was away. Word reached Lulu Lee of the rumor that Charles was having a dalliance with their "house guest," Dorothy. The bonds of love were so strong between Charles and Lulu Lee, that Idalynn and her mother were both shocked at such accusations, and dismissed such talk from their minds, as poppycock!

————————

Upon returning to Lexington, Lulu Lee found that Dorothy was gone. It was most unlikely that Dorothy would have left their home without saying good-bye to Lulu Lee, but Charles told Lulu Lee that Dorothy had acquired another position, a position for which Lulu Lee had been grooming her. Lulu Lee was happy for Dorothy.

Back in Chicago, Idalynn, Michael and baby, Lee, appeared to be the perfect young family. With the assistance of a full-time nursemaid, Idalynn was adjusting to motherhood quite well. There was a deep sense of peace within Idalynn—perhaps maybe a peace of submission.

For Idalynn, it was a joy to hold the baby or to rock her to sleep. When the baby needed attention, or when it wasn't convenient for Idalynn to be disturbed, she had a nursemaid, upon whom to rely.

It was only when the baby did something cute or new did Idalynn wish that she had her mother there to see it too. In the back of Idalynn's mind, memories of Lexington were resurfacing. Idalynn's thoughts always traveled back to the time in her life, when she had been the happiest—in Lexington. During her solitary moments, she knew she wanted that life back.

Dark Days

The months passed quickly. In the eyes of her parents, Lee grew more and more adorable with each day. All too soon, the baby was walking about the apartment and expressing her every desire. Lee had definitely assumed her place as a real member within the family.

Charles and Lulu Lee spoke with Idalynn every Sunday afternoon, and Charles was especially delighted to carry on conversations with little Lee. Throughout the week, Lulu Lee sent articles of interest clipped from the Lexington newspaper. Unknown to her mother, every time Idalynn read of Lexington activities, she became very morose.

While the Spencers in Lexington had a very active social life, Michael was busy and successful with his work in Chicago of chasing down the criminals. Idalynn felt as though she was the only member of the family that was devoid of anything interesting in her life. While she possessed an obsession for the love of her little girl, she possessed the same intensity of callous disregard for Michael's career.

Michael, trying to calm the fears that Idalynn had for the career that he had chosen, suggested to Idalynn that they leave the Chicago area, and move to Wisconsin. Michael felt that, by living in Milwaukee, it would still be possible for him to commute to Chicago where he needed to be. And, too, his parents lived nearby to assist if necessary.

Idalynn looked upon Wisconsin as the place where elephants go to die, and refused to even consider a move there. In actuality, Idalynn did not want to be under the scrutiny of Michael's parents. There was no consoling Idalynn. To make matters even worse, Idalynn was out of sorts and not feeling well. She blamed the nausea that she was experiencing on Chicago's poor air quality. All too soon, Idalynn realized a second child was on the way.

Of course, Lulu Lee and Charles were once again overjoyed. Their family was growing. They remembered when their doctor at Idalynn's birth had told them that they could never have future children. Now a second baby on the way in Idalynn's family, was making up for some of those sad days that they had experienced themselves.

Idalynn was not well and had been advised by her doctor that traveling on a jerky train to go back to Lexington was out of the question. Lulu Lee advised her that she could not leave Charles at this time to come to Chicago, but she would be counting the months when she, once again, would meet the newest grandchild.

Idalynn thought it was so unlike her mother not to jump at the chance to come to Chicago immediately to see them. She entertained the question in her mind if all was well in Lexington.

Time progressed and it was drawing closer to the arrival of the expected baby. Lulu Lee was preparing the house so that she would be ready to leave on her trip to Chicago, when Michael called to tell her that little Emily, named for his mother, had arrived. Lulu Lee was so happy! Although, this was an unexpected early arrival date, Lulu Lee assured Michael that she would arrive in Chicago within a few hours to assist in any manner that she could. Michael told his mother-in-law that they would manage well until she got there, as his mother was also planning to drive in from Milwaukee, just a little more than an hour away.

Idalynn asked Michael, "Did you tell your mother when you spoke with her on the phone that my mother was on her way? What I mean is, it will not be necessary for her to upset her lifestyle by staying any length of time." Idalynn added quickly, "Of course, I am anxious for her to see our baby. I just don't want her to plan to stay very long."

Not wanting to take the conversation any further, Michael responded, "Yes Idalynn. I understand what you are saying."

Lulu Lee scurried about the house before leaving Lexington to be with Idalynn and the children. She assured herself that Charles would be able to manage while she was away.

Driving Lulu Lee to the train station, Charles said, "I am so happy for all of us. We have a wonderful son-in-law, and now, two wonderful grandchildren. You, Lulu Lee are responsible for all of our happiness. I love you more today than ever before. I shall miss you so much while you are away from me. Spare no expense. Please call me frequently to tell me everything about the family." Lulu Lee felt that she was the luckiest woman in the world. She had it all!

Arriving in Chicago, Lulu Lee found Idalynn to be feeling well and emotionally upbeat. Idalynn felt having her mother with her was the ultimate feeling of happiness. Michael was extremely proud of his two little girls, and seemed to walk with a spring in his step.

In the meantime, Michael's mother had decided that she would save her visit for another time when her daughter-in-law really needed her. She asked Michael if it was possible that Idalynn could send some pictures of both children so she didn't feel completely excluded. She understood all too well.

Charles sent a rocking horse for baby Emily, and a set of play dishes for two-year old, Lee. The card enclosed said, "For my two special babies. Love, Daddy Spencer."

"Daddy Spencer" was the name that Charles had bestowed upon himself. Charles was anxious for the day when both children would call him by that name. For now though, he was just elated that indirectly, there were two more Spencers!

———————

It was while Lulu Lee was in Chicago that once again, rumors reached Lulu Lee alluding to Charles enjoying the company of another woman. Lulu Lee's friend even went so far as to mention that the woman was much younger than she. Lulu Lee preferred not to dignify these rumors by addressing them to Charles, but Lulu Lee was definitely hurting.

Upon returning home to Lexington, Lulu Lee was told by her friends of more rumors pertaining to Charles and this woman. In a flash of anger, Lulu Lee phoned the woman in question and had a lengthy and shocking conversation.

Lulu Lee confronted Charles when he returned home from work that evening. At first Charles was steadfast in denying all of the accusations.

"Charles," Lulu Lee began, "I have at this time spoken with your "friend," (Lulu Lee refusing to give her the courtesy of using her name). In her defensive mode, she spoke freely of intimate details of the manner in which you both conducted yourselves. She spared me no details! She has told me that you said that you loved her, as she did you."

While Charles was pleading with Lulu Lee to forgive him, Lulu Lee asked Charles, "Do you remember the promise that you made, not only to me, but to my parents as well, of keeping love, devotion and decency in our marriage?" Lulu Lee went on to say, "I am just so thankful that both of my parents did not live to see this day!"

Charles pleaded, "Lulu Lee, I cannot change the past. I beg you. Let me control the future. Forgive me."

Lulu Lee was simply too devastated and confused to entertain any such idea of forgiveness or to continue living with him. Unfaithfulness was something that was unacceptable to her. Lulu Lee knew that at times people do deceive one another, even those whom they love the most. For now though, Lulu Lee felt the truth was more than she could bear to hear. She wanted to believe that she had always been Charles' "one and only" since she was sixteen years old.

During the next several weeks, Lulu Lee constantly heard additional rumors linking Charles to not one woman, but several. It was said that Charles had engaged in more than one imprudent romance. It was now apparent to her that Charles not only had an insatiable appetite for prestige, but also women. Betrayal was the word that occupied her feelings and thoughts.

Charles was the talk of her social circles. She was spoken about as the betrayed wife. It was demeaning to her to accept sympathy from her loyal friends. She questioned to herself, "Who among her friends had also been with her husband?"

Not being able to endure the heartbreak, and the dread of facing all the humiliation, Lulu Lee knew she would have to hold her head high and move on with life. With the bonds of love for Charles slowly unraveling before her eyes, Lulu Lee held no illusions. The dream of living with Charles forever would now remain just that—a dream. She believed that her marriage was broken beyond hope.

Grave Resolutions

With Idalynn's strong denunciation of her father's affairs, she begged her mother to leave her father, and move to Chicago, to be closer to her. Lulu Lee was torn. She did not know where her loyalties lay. Knowing that Idalynn was not emotionally able to accept her life in Chicago, or able to care for two babies, Lulu Lee felt she was more needed by her daughter. After all, hadn't Charles brought this upon himself? With this uppermost in her thoughts, she was faced with making an agonizing decision.

Knowing her marriage to Charles was irreconcilable, and against Charles' wishes, Lulu Lee separated from Charles. Lulu Lee knew in her heart that the time of fulfilling any future dreams with Charles was over. The life that she had lived in Lexington was gone. For now, her plans were to put all her emotional energies into moving to Chicago and assist in raising her grandbabies. Lulu Lee and Pat Bailey, the dog, prepared to move.

Charles was brimming with anger with Idalynn, who had always had his complete devotion, and who was now encouraging his wife to leave him. With his raging temper, he retaliated by calling his attorney to draws up a writ to disown his only child, as well as her children. Charles thought to himself, *if his family wanted to live apart from him, he would definitely make it a point not to be a part of them!* He had his vast business holdings directed elsewhere.

Idalynn knew her father could be very explosive at times, like herself. She knew well his anger would subside. She was not concerned. She was just pleased that things had gone her way, and her mother would now be by her side. Idalynn felt that her father had broken his vows to her mother. He deserved to be alone. Michael found it best to remain silent in this matter. He prepared himself to watch it play out.

The void, created by Lulu Lee's absence in Charles' life, would never be completely filled again. Charles' grief would never disappear, and he could only hope that time would lessen the pain. After several months of being alone, hearing nothing from Lulu Lee, Charles made a heart-wrenching decision. Charles petitioned the courts for a five-year legal separation. Surely, he thought, that this would allow time for Lulu Lee's anger to subside. He wanted forgiveness and to move forward in mending his broken marriage, rather than rush into a divorce.

Lulu Lee never answered the court's petition, during the entire five-year separation. She let the divorce action take its course. She adored her grandbabies and knew that Idalynn was incapable of raising the babies. It was her plan never to return to Charles, or her lovely home, again. She only asked for certain pieces of her furniture and her mother's china.

———————

After five years, with nothing to go on, the courts reinstated "bachelorhood" to Charles, and petitioned Charles to pay Lulu Lee a substantial amount of money on which to live. Lulu Lee walked away from a life with Charles and her lovely home on Versailles Parkway. She had departed from a very gracious lifestyle, but she did have her grandbabies. Charles, in the meantime, was paying a terrible price for his philandering.

With no contact from Lulu Lee during the past five years, Charles could only assume that Lulu Lee was where she wanted to be, leading the life that she wanted in an apartment upstairs from Idalynn. Still he felt it appropriate to tell Lulu Lee of his plans to remarry. Penning a letter, he wanted her to know that even though he was moving forward with his life, he would always be around to assist her, should she need him. Charles emphasized to Lulu Lee that he never wanted to cut the bonds between them. He said, "In my heart Lulu Lee, I love you very much and always will."

———————————

Within several months, one of Lulu Lee's friends in Lexington sent her a short newspaper clipping announcing Charles' marriage to a woman from Tennessee. Lulu Lee could not help but reminisce about the time in her life when she was a young girl and had initially met Charles. She had been so proud to take him home to Mulberry where she had lived on her family's farm and in time, would be where their marriage would take place. Now she was living in an up-stairs apartment in Chicago. She had left behind the social world she had previously known. Lulu Lee's thoughts were tearing her apart. "What have I done?"

In time, word drifted to Lulu Lee that Charles and his new wife had opened a creamery in Horse Cave on Water Street. Lulu Lee was saddened as she remembered that these had been their plans so many years ago. Horse Cave was her home and she could not help but feel that Charles had violated something sacred to her. This was to have been her spiritual connection to her mother, Angeline. This business adventure of Charles' made her inconsolable. "Oh Charles, what happened to us?"

Independent Lives

Michael's involvement with his career of tracking down criminals caused him to be away from home the majority of the time. It was comforting to him, to know that Lulu Lee was playing such a positive part in Idalynn's and the children's lives, while he was away. It was obvious to all that Lulu Lee was exuding a powerful, matriarchal air over the entire Brooks family. Although Lulu Lee cherished the role that she played, it was all she really had. Hearing Idalynn call her mother, "Mama," prompted the children to call Lulu Lee, "Mama," as well. Idalynn was called "Mother." The bonds of dependency between Idalynn and her mother were growing even stronger.

Lulu Lee's devotion to the grandchildren never wavered. It was she who provided the children with emotional stability. Whoever the children were to become began during those formative years under the sole care of "Mama." With Lulu Lee being the leading presence in the home, Idalynn was afforded much free time of her own.

Idalynn seemed remarkably different. She was cultivating new friends and creating a new life. At times, it seemed as though Idalynn was living in her own self-absorbed world—detached from her family, always having some place to go. For Idalynn, these were busy and happy days!

Back in Lexington, Charles decided it was in his best interest to leave the business of the Spencer Brothers in the hands of his two younger brothers. Whether from uneasy feelings from his brothers regarding his recent remarriage, or perhaps knowledge that his new wife was being shunned by his previous society friends, Charles decided to leave his roots in Kentucky, and to move to Tennessee, the home state of his wife.

Irrespective of his new marriage, Charles and Lulu Lee maintained a deep friendship and an unspoken understanding of each other. Charles continued to remind Lulu Lee that she would always be able to rely on him. Lulu Lee knew she could.

As the months passed, Idalynn had a very difficult time trying to resolve her anger toward her father for his having caused so much pain to her mother. Consequently, she chose to walk away from her father, rather than try to forgive him or to endear herself to him. She was not interested in seeing her father with his new wife standing by his side. He, on the other hand, showed no interest or made any plans to meet with her. A healing process was just not happening between them. Charles made no provisions to meet his two little grandchildren. He also was not aware that a third little grandchild was on the way. As far he was concerned, Idalynn and children did not exist.

Discord in the Family

Michael and Idalynn continued to have strong arguments with one another. Michael accused Idalynn of being more devoted to her new circle of friends than to her own family. It was apparent to him that she was spending less and less time at home. It was also apparent to Michael that the children were becoming more attached to their grandmother, than to their mother. There was no question in Michael's mind that Idalynn was taking a radical approach to this marriage.

There were times, when Lulu Lee would rush the children out of range to avoid hearing the arguments between their parents. In one particular fit of rage, Idalynn told Michael that she wanted a divorce—in spite of the fact that she was pregnant.

Michael demanded, "Idalynn, calm yourself. It isn't good for you or our expected baby to be so upset!"

Idalynn, with her passion so inflamed, angrily replied, "What makes you think this baby is yours? You're never at home!" At that moment, Michael threw a cup of hot coffee in Idalynn's face.

Michael was shocked, and confused, and angry with himself, for having behaved in the manner that he had. Her statement concerning the baby, puzzled him. He questioned in his mind, *how did he miss knowing things were so bad?* Now he wondered whether Idalynn was speaking the truth, or was it a desperate plea by her for him to recognize that he needed to spend more time with his family. He wanted to think the latter.

John Taylor

One of Idalynn's and Michael's friends was a prominent radio announcer in the Chicago area. His name was John Taylor. John, Michael and Idalynn had always been good friends, and always seemed to enjoy being in one another's company. John was outgoing and possessed a delightful nature, always creating laughter whenever he was in a group. At the same time, he was a cultured and charming man.

Idalynn found enjoyment in her relationship with John; he was just the opposite of the serious and quiet side of her own husband. Over the course of time, John and Idalynn realized the bonds of attraction were growing stronger between them. Idalynn had allowed John to move into her heart. If truth were told, Idalynn felt herself to be deeply in love with John.

With Michael being away so much of the time, John was escorting Idalynn, with Michael's acquiescence, to various social affairs that Michael and Idalynn were obligated to support. Eventually, infatuation and even love, replaced Idalynn's loneliness.

John and Idalynn believed that without one another, life would be meaningless. For Idalynn, it was a golden time. It was obvious that Idalynn had not fallen far from the "Mighty Oak." What she condemned in her father was now a part of her own life. Idalynn preferred not to accept that she was indeed a reflection of her father.

When Idalynn told John that she was pregnant with his child, he insisted she divorce Michael as quickly as possible, so they could be married. He promised her he would take care of her and the children. John said, "Idalynn, marry me, and I will buy you one of the loveliest homes in Chicago, and you will want for nothing! You will live a life of luxury."

As Idalynn was immersed in deep thought about her future, a future that subsequently did not include Michael, she realized that marrying John and living in Chicago was not what she really wanted at all. She wanted to live in Lexington! She wondered how she could convince John to continue his radio career in Lexington. Also to consider, John hadn't mentioned anything about her mother living with them. Whatever would she do without her mother? She wondered if John would welcome Mama into their home?

Idalynn needed to have definite questions answered. In the back of her mind, she was beginning to have misgivings about John. She asked herself, *was it possible that she and John were involved in just a painful love affair?* Calling John, they agreed to meet at the entrance of Marshall Fields Department Store on State Street. In the event anyone was to see them, it would be quite plausible that they had accidentally bumped into one another, while she was shopping.

They agreed to meet at two o'clock that afternoon.

By two o'clock, John had not arrived. As the minutes passed, Idalynn became somewhat agitated. She wondered if perhaps John had changed his mind. Perhaps, he was having second thoughts about marrying her, (as she was him) and acquiring a ready-made family. Where was he? she asked herself.

At three o'clock, Idalynn annoyingly boarded the Chicago Elevated Railroad to return home. Upon reaching home, she put a call in to John at his office. When his secretary answered, Idalynn asked to speak with Mr. Taylor, identifying herself as a reporter from *The Chicago Tribune*.

The secretary, feeling anyone from the news department should be advised of the tragedy that had befallen all of them, said, "Mr. Taylor had a luncheon engagement with a friend, this afternoon, and upon leaving the luncheon to go to another meeting, he was struck and killed by a taxi cab as he was crossing the street. He would have been thirty-eight years old tomorrow. We are all so distraught!"

Not able to process what the secretary was saying, and not wanting to hear what she was hearing, Idalynn hung up the telephone in a state of panic and complete confusion. She could not believe what she had just heard. "Of course, this could not be true! How could this have happened? Surely, there must be some mistake. Maybe it was all a bad dream." She started to shake uncontrollably and her sobbing took over her entire body.

It seemed like an eternity of being alone in her room, when Idalynn heard knocking on her apartment door. "Idalynn, its Mama," called Lulu Lee. When her mother let herself in the door, she asked, "Idalynn, why is it so dark in here? I've tried calling you so many times, but your line has been busy."

Idalynn was disoriented and quickly tried to compose herself. Turning on some lights, she noticed that the phone was off the cradle. Apparently, she had not hung the phone up properly, after having talked to John's office. And then the horrible thought re-entered her mind. There was no John, anymore. She felt as though she were living in a nightmare!

Lulu Lee said, "I've fed the children and they're upstairs playing. I must not be gone from them too long—maybe just a minute or two." Idalynn, nonchalantly mentioned that she had been shopping when she felt ill, so returned home to lie down, and must have fallen into a deep sleep.

Lulu Lee said, "Idalynn, the evening news on the radio said John Taylor, yours and Michael's friend, was killed this afternoon. He was struck by a taxicab. The station said there would be more details with later newscasts."

Idalynn said, "Oh no, Mama, surely not!" She broke down and started to sob hysterically. Lulu Lee could not help but notice the profound degree of suffering that her daughter seemed to be experiencing. Although Lulu Lee was saddened as well, she thought it was most out of the ordinary that Idalynn should be so affected with such deep grief. For Idalynn, however, the reality of it all had finally settled upon her.

Desperation

The front door opened and Michael walked in. Lulu Lee looked up and said, "Oh Michael, Idalynn and I were just discussing John Taylor's death. Isn't it just dreadful?"

"Yes, Mama," said Michael, "I had just had lunch with John earlier today, shortly before the accident." Idalynn paled. She couldn't envision for what reason, the two of them were having lunch, on the very day that she too was meeting with John. Idalynn wondered, *Surely, John wasn't discussing her?*

Idalynn quickly interjected, "The last time I saw John was about two months ago, when we all dined at the Palmer House. I didn't dream that that would be the last time that I would ever see him." Tears welled up in her eyes.

Michael did not offer to comfort Idalynn, but walked into the bedroom to change his clothes. Lulu Lee excused herself, not only to return to her grandchildren upstairs, but also, because she felt negative feelings developing between her daughter and Michael.

Idalynn followed Michael into the bedroom, and perhaps out of desperation and fear of how the next few moments would play out said, "Michael, I know this is such a tragedy, and we will both miss John dreadfully; but for now, we must try to move through this sorrowful event. It is a difficult time for all of us, but we must remember the good times with him. More importantly, we must concentrate on our new baby and appreciate our lives together."

Michael, who dearly idolized Idalynn, put his arms around her and told her how much he was looking forward to the expected baby. He told her how much he loved her and his girls. He said, "Maybe, if we have a boy, we could name him after John."

Idalynn, thought to herself of the irony of that statement. She was also wondering and worried over what John and Michael might have discussed during luncheon that day. Idalynn knew that it was possible that her marriage was in a very precarious position.

Idalynn and Michael talked late into the night. Idalynn appeared to have a complete change of attitude. She wanted to say what Michael wanted to hear. She even proposed moving to Milwaukee to be nearer his parents, if that is what he wanted. Idalynn knew she had no bargaining power. More importantly, she didn't want to be the topic of discussions among their acquaintances, should rumors start to circulate.

Michael, wanting the children to know his own mother, as they did her mother, thought a move to Milwaukee was a positive idea. Idalynn, on the other hand, just wanted to leave the Chicago area. Lulu Lee, believing she knew more than she was being told, could not help but think, that this was the second time that she would be moving to another strange city. Reluctantly on Lulu Lee's part, plans were set into motion to move to Wisconsin, after the baby was born.

Wisconsin

A baby girl arrived and was named Suzanne. Although Michael had had a mindset of having a son, he was thrilled to have a healthy baby daughter once again. With Michael's life busily occupied with his commuting from his home in Milwaukee to his work in Chicago, Lulu Lee's presence in their home was greatly appreciated. He also knew that Lulu Lee cherished every moment whenever she could be a part of Idaynn's life.

The benefits were enormous for all. With Lulu Lee once again running the household, Idalynn found herself with much free time, allowing her to be a playmate to her children. The children were so fortunate to be receiving love and attention from their Mama, and both of their parents.

The down-side of having too little to occupy her time was, although Idalynn was making every effort to make friends with the ladies in the neighborhood, she found none to be very stimulating. She just wasn't interested in recipes or shopping for bargains in the grocery store. When she introduced conversations regarding make-up or graceful styles of clothing or even furniture, she found none of the women particularly interested. Again, she found herself having a difficult time in adjusting to her new surroundings. Again, she was lonely.

Michael's mother, Emma, trying to establish a relationship with both Idalynn and Lulu Lee, offered to teach Idalynn several domesticities, but Idalynn was repulsed by the whole idea. Idalynn said, "Emma, I have been raised as a Southern lady; and Southern ladies usually have others to do those sorts of thing for them."

Lulu Lee too, became aware of the disadvantages of living in Milwaukee. Michael's mother was continuing to drop by their home to visit, and Lulu Lee and Idalynn did not enjoy what they thought to be meaningless and empty conversations. While at their home, Emma would offer varied suggestions of better ways to run a household, as well as better methods of raising the children. Lulu Lee was most affronted!

Idalynn took great pride in her three little girls and dressed them in "Shirley Temple" frocks. Michael's mother, upon seeing the children dressed as such, said the dresses were a waste of Michael's money. Lulu Lee took much care in curling the children's hair every day. She painstakingly brushed each curl around her finger, with a brush dipped in hair gel, until she had created a Shirley Temple type of hairstyle—the style of the time.

Michael's mother said that the children would be much neater in appearance if they wore their hair in braids. Idalynn was a constant irritation to Michael's mother and Idalynn enjoyed every moment of it!

Although, Lulu Lee and Idalynn appeared to be living a life of normalcy, they both felt that they were living in a distasteful locale and were both feeling despondent with life in general in Milwaukee. They were Southerners, and detested living even further north than Chicago. They both felt they were merely existing.

A Passage in Time

At first, Michael thought his wife's restlessness was part of being so involved with the three little children that she had no time for outside activities. After discussing it with Lulu Lee, Michael suggested to Idalynn that she should take a short vacation, just for a change of scenery.

Idalynn thought it over, and discussed it with her mother, as to whether or not she would mind if she went to visit her father. With Lulu Lee's encouragement to go, she discussed her plans with Michael. Michael thought it was a wonderful idea, thinking to himself that it was important for Idalynn and her father to reconcile.

Idalynn wrote to her father, proposing a visit to him. Charles wrote in return that he was pleased to hear from her, and that she was most welcome. Idalynn was hoping that this visit with her father might mend some fences between them. Idalynn wanted all the past ill feelings to merely become a part of a passage of time, not a place forever. In the meantime, Charles was looking forward to her arrival. He quietly wondered to himself how Lulu Lee was doing.

Lulu Lee was very skeptical of anything positive coming out of this meeting between Charles and Idalynn, but Idalynn desperately held out optimism. Michael took Idalynn to the train station for her trip to Columbia, Tennessee, where Charles and his wife lived. Michael suggested to Idalynn to let the past rest, and to try not to feel ill will toward her father's second wife. In her heart, Idalynn planned to feign anything, rather than set her eyes upon her!

Arriving in Columbia, Idalynn was met at the train station by her father. It was a deeply emotional meeting, as they had not seen one another in almost nine years. After Idalynn greeted her father and told him how much she had missed him, Charles said, "There is much that needs to be said, and many misconceptions that need to be resolved." Then Charles added, "We have your room waiting for you at home."

With that remark, a barrier was erected. Idalynn, never one to mince words, said with an icy arrogance, "Daddy, I know it is not what you have planned, but please, I insist that you take me to a hotel. I really choose not to come face to face with Mama's replacement!"

Charles bristled and said, "I forbid you to speak to me in that tone! Under the circumstances, and the mood that you have just established, I am only too glad to find accommodations for you in a hotel! I was hoping that our visit together would be a wonderful time. Perhaps, I have hoped in error."

Silently, Charles drove Idalynn to a down-town hotel. Upon arriving, he assisted her in checking in, and told the clerk to direct bill her room and amenities to him at his company, Kentucky Cheeses, Inc.

Sitting down with Idalynn in the lobby, Charles turned to Idalynn and said, "My daughter, much has transpired in our lifetime to create dark depths, and our family life certainly suffered, but please do not plan to lecture or to place blame. I made a grievous mistake. I didn't realize then what I was about to lose. Please know that I was always completely devoted to you and to your mother."

Continuing, Charles said, "I watched your mother grow from a coltish young girl to an elegant woman. Over the years, I gave her cause to leave me and to be close to you and Michael. Eventually, my tears dried and disappeared, but quiet tears still come when I least expect them, whenever I think of your mother.

Now, I believe that I have said enough on that subject. I have no further comments to make regarding my past life. Let's get on with making up for lost time. I'll have a car come by and pick you up in the morning to bring you to the plant. Just call, whenever you are ready."

When Idalynn retired that evening, memories of her life surfaced regarding when they were all together, living in Lexington. She felt so homesick for her past life. With her always-present obsession to return permanently to Lexington, she felt only then would she be completely happy.

Idalynn loved her father very much. He had always paved the way for her to excel, making so many excuses for her, even when she showed inexcusable behavior. She recognized the fact that her father had always made it possible for her to have the best that life had to offer. In her heart, she could not point a finger at him now for any of his past actions. She knew exactly, by virtue of her own actions in her own marriage, how emotions do sometimes run wild.

Locked away in her mind was a plan. She knew it would not be difficult at all to persuade her mother to return to Lexington, as Mama was only in Wisconsin because of her and the children. The only uncertain detail was Michael. Would he follow? She told herself that she really didn't care if he didn't! However, should there be a divorce, she wondered if she would need Michael's permission to take the children out of the state of Wisconsin.

The three-day visit with her father turned out to be a meaningful and calm experience. Father and daughter enjoyed long conversations, and even laughter. When it was time to return home to Milwaukee, Idalynn felt more love and compassion, as well as understanding, toward her father than she had in many years. She knew she would miss him dearly. She also questioned her own actions as to why she had allowed so many years to pass without being close to him. More importantly, as a result of this visit with her father, Idalynn had a clearer vision of what she needed to do.

Speaking to her father about her unhappiness with living in Milwaukee, as well as her deteriorating relationship with Michael, Idalynn told her father that she was thinking of leaving him.

The only reaction from her father was when he said to her, "Idalynn, ultimately you must find your own way in life. I encourage you to take control of this sad situation, and try to make things right. I know my own grief from my own mistakes will never end. If you divorce Michael, you must accept whatever fate awaits you. You then will have to live with any consequences."

Although Idalynn never agreed to meet Charles' wife, "the replacement," during her stay in Columbia, Idalynn felt that the time she had spent with her father had been wonderful!

Torment

Back home with the children and Lulu Lee, Idalynn informed her mother of her plans to divorce Michael, and to return to Lexington. Lulu Lee begged, "Oh, Idalynn, for the sake of the children, please, come to your senses!" Idalynn was adamant. Lulu Lee was distraught, just thinking about all the consequences of this. She asked herself, *What about my grandbabies? What would happen to them? Would Michael even permit the children to leave the state or worse, would he win full custody of the children?* Being an attorney, Lulu Lee feared Michael would have all the right moves to make things go his way.

For the first time in her life, Lulu Lee knew that, if forced to make a decision between her daughter and her grandchildren, she would choose her grandchildren. Her passion in life now, was to care for the babies. She would, if necessary, choose to remain in Milwaukee, to be with them. Lulu Lee became physically ill!

When Michael returned home from Chicago that evening, Idalynn asked him to sit down, as she had something very serious to discuss with him.

"Michael," Idalynn began, "I simply am not tolerating living here in Milwaukee. I have given serious thought to my situation, Michael, and I frankly feel that we need to separate, and probably, eventually divorce. Believe me when I insist. I want to be fair to you, to Mama, and to the children. I want a better life for us all, including you."

Michael was not expecting this from Idalynn. He adamantly said to Idalynn, "There will absolutely be no divorce! I love my three little girls too much to ever be apart from them! Never would I allow anyone to take them out of my life! I strongly suggest that you rethink your irrational and "fair" plans! If you persist, you may leave—but, without the children!"

Then Idalynn screamed." Michael, Don't talk about your three little girls! Suzanne is not your child! She belongs to John Taylor!" Michael angrily glared at her, saying nothing. He was shocked that she would even allude to the baby! He questioned to himself, *Just how emotionally off balance was Idalynn?*

Michael begged Lulu Lee to intervene, and stop the hysteria that was being played out, but Idalynn would not relent. With her fiery temper, she said, "I intend to divorce you, Michael!" Michael, with clenched fists was trying desperately to control his anger. "What about your pledge of fidelity to me?" Michael yelled.

Reeling from emotions of shock and anger, Michael felt his life was veering toward disaster. He knew he would have to fight with everything he had to keep his family intact, but even he was concerned with the chances of how the chips would fall in winning this battle. It was as though he didn't know this woman and certainly couldn't understand her thinking. Michael questioned himself as to why Idalynn couldn't be happy with him. Locked in the back of his mind, Michael regretted not spending more time at home. He realized that he had to accept some of the responsibility of this profound situation.

The next few days, Lulu Lee moved silently and apprehensively about the home, busying herself caring for the children. She only prayed that all this upheaval would resolve itself without too much volatility in the household. When Idalynn contacted a divorce lawyer, Lulu Lee knew that it would only be a matter of time before they would all be in upheaval—again.

The wheels were set into motion. Having passed the bar in three states, Illinois, Indiana and Kentucky, Michael was well known among his peers, and had a reputation for having sound and fair judgment. Inwardly, Michael vowed to himself that Idalynn would rue the day for her indiscretion.

Feeling in his own mind that his wife was unstable, he asked two of his fellow attorneys to represent him in court. He asked the attorneys to take a deposition from his wife, make up their own minds regarding testimony received from her, and report their findings to the court.

With a subpoena in hand, an officer of the court called upon Idalynn to summons her to meet with Michael's attorney. Most reluctantly she agreed to do so, thinking that she may as well get this over. It was to her thinking that people may as well know how impossible it was to share a life with

Michael. Machine guns and disappearing acts for days—or longer, were not to her liking in a marriage.

A few days after the meeting, Idalynn received a special delivery letter in the mail, with a formal request for her to come to a medical clinic for an evaluation as to her being a sound and fit mother for their children. Idalynn, shredding the document, ignored it.

With this uncooperative action from Idalynn, as well as her not responding to their orders, the court served her notice that she was to be committed to a mental hospital for thirty days where she would receive the evaluation that they had wanted. Idalynn knew that Michael was at the root of this persecution of her, because of John Taylor.

Contacting legal advice, Idalynn's lawyer testified in court, "It was possible that Idalynn Brooks had ignored, or suppressed her responsibilities as a mother, but never were her children put in harm's way. Her mother, Lulu Lee Spencer, had always been in the home with the children. Surely, Mr. Brooks will attest to that."

Idalynn's attorney went on to say, "Idalynn had indeed been involved in an illicit romance, as her marriage to Michael Brooks had always been a mismatch, and consequently, a tempestuous and stormy relationship. I have witnesses who will attest to that. I am, at this time, petitioning the courts to allow Idalynn the privilege of a divorce so that she might concentrate on a private life without Michael Brooks."

Michael Brooks, who was known to be of high moral character, along with his charismatic demeanor, took the stand and painted a controversial portrait of a woman who was reckless and abrasive and who had never grown to adulthood. Michael said, "Idalynn was euphoric one day and filled with apprehensions the next day. I can only conclude that my wife is definitely unstable and a possible threat to my children's safety." Michael was pulling out all the stops.

The court sent down a message that in the best interest of the children, it was necessary to find out which of the two parties was correct in their assessment of Idalynn Brooks. In order to do so, Mrs. Brooks would have to submit to a thirty-day observation period in the state hospital for evaluation.

Against the advice from her attorney, Idalynn absolutely refused to (volunteer on her own) enter the state hospital in Waupon. Consequently, a "writ of seizure" was enacted. When the attendants came to Idalynn's home to escort her to the hospital, Idalynn screamed "I absolutely will not agree to this. I refuse to leave!" The attendants pulled out a straight jacket to use on her. "Please don't put a straight jacket on me in view of my children and my mother! Don't touch me!" Unwilling to walk to the van, Idalynn was dragged forcibly from her home, struggling and crying and taken against her will, to the mental hospital.

Michael was unnerved when he heard this, as he had not meant for things to go this far. Lulu Lee, not only had not wanted the three children to see this horrible scene, she could not bear to see her daughter's pain and anguish. There was such an indignity of being confined in a sanitarium. Lulu Lee was very angry with Michael, but was afraid to express herself, for fear, that the children would be taken from her. She wondered how he could be so cruel and insensitive. She suspected that Michael had used his political power, and "called in" some favors due him. Lulu Lee called Charles, immediately!

Joining Forces

Charles and Lulu Lee joined forces. Charles called Michael, and in a less than a gentle manner, threatened him, stating he would use all his power to make certain that Michael would never see his children again if he persisted in this manner toward Idalynn. Charles insisted that Michael go to the courts, and in some manner have this indignant writ against his daughter rescinded.

Michael said to Charles, "What I have done, needed to be done. You are remiss in not knowing all of the details. Because I love my children and know that they will have excellent care with my mother-in-law, I will offer Spencer custody of my children to her. Charles, should you persist any longer in these matters, I will give custody to my own mother." Charles was not use to this type of condescending attitude toward himself. Retaliating, he threatened Michael with bodily harm.

Lulu Lee pleaded with Charles, "Charles, please don't pursue this matter any further. I would not be able to bear it if Michael took my grandbabies away from me."

Although Charles was not able to override the courts "Statue of Confinement" for Idalynn, he was able to have her confinement period reduced to twenty-one days. Tests were to be administered to determine her state of mind. It was felt that Idalynn needed to confront her past.

Idalynn's stay in the hospital consisted of what was called, "light therapy." She found herself painting, singing, reading, even making mud pies—all the things that she had taught the little children in her kindergarten classes in her earlier life. Looking around at some of the other inmates, Idalynn could not help but think there was a distinguishing innocence, associated with mental illness that was sad.

Twenty-one days later, Idalynn was released from the mental institution, still wearing the mandatory, blue striped cotton inmate dress. With her spunk and determination, Idalynn was able to survive her time in the institution quite well. Again, with her charm and witty personality, the attendants there thought her to be a very nice lady and a delight to have as a guest!

Medical tests offered a diagnosis that Idalynn was a sociopath—one who has no sense of moral obligation, whatsoever, to others. Records showed that Idalynn possessed a brain with crossed wiring, causing the brain to lose control and resulting in a tortured mind of delusions. Doctors at the institution went so far as to say that they were in agreement that her present condition denoted that she was unbalanced, perhaps even insane. The prognosis was that she was not mentally or morally responsible for herself, but in time, with proper medication and supervision, Idalynn could conquer herself and would be a normal person one day. Since she did not show any evidence of suicidal or homicidal tendencies, she was released to the care and custody of her mother, Lulu Lee Spencer.

There was such a profound dejection within Idalynn. While she was astonished what the medical profession had labeled her it was the social stigma of having been in a sanitarium that bothered her the most. Her mother, on the other hand, told her daughter, "Idalynn, don't dwell on the past. Our future with the children is what matters. We are blessed to have our babies."

The doctor explained to Michael and Lulu Lee that this personality disorder usually stemmed from an emotionally deprived childhood, as well as not having been held accountable for any of her own actions. Punishment or incarceration would not be of any help. He continued his conversation by saying, "Idalynn is a case of needing much supervision, along with much shown love, to assist her in not acting out impulsively or irresponsibly."

Within her own heart, Lulu Lee knew her daughter did have issues that needed to be resolved. It was just unfathomable in her mind that she and Charles had neglected Idalynn in any manner. They had given her all that she ever desired. Lulu Lee was so bewildered that she turned and walked away from the doctor, tears streaming down her face.

Michael was not wrong in recognizing this in Idalynn. Michael insisted that what he did was for Idalynn's own safety. He said, "I meant well." Idalynn would not acknowledge Michael's sentiments. She told anyone who would listen, that she hated him! Michael was the enemy.

Divorce

Surprising to none, Idalynn started divorce proceedings immediately. She charged extreme cruelty! Michael countered with the charge of adultery—but he offered no proof. He merely wanted Idalynn to know that he was never unaware of her marital behavior. It was mandated that, until further hearings, that Idalynn could not leave the state with the children. Michael, by nature of his job, could go wherever he was needed, even with the children.

The first repercussion of the divorce proceedings was when the judge took the three children into his chambers and asked each of them, with which parent they preferred to live. Lee, at ten years of age, unequivocally said, "Mother." Although, she knew she was the apple of her Daddy's eye, she would never detach herself from Mama, Lulu Lee.

Emily chose "Mother," knowing well that was where Mama would be. In later years, Emily would say that she felt she had betrayed her father, for answering in that manner. Suzanne, at five years old, chose "Mother." Suzanne would always do whatever her six-year-old sister would do. Suzanne too worried, "Will Daddy be angry with me?"

Six months later, a divorce was granted to Idalynn, but to Idalynn's shock, full custody of the children was given to Michael.

Michael, agreeing to give joint custody of the children to Idalynn's household, said, "Not wanting to cause my children anymore disruption to their lives, and by virtue of my career, I am not able to be at home a great deal, I will allow their grandmother, Lulu Lee Spencer to have joint custody of my children, for the interim. However, I want the courts to instruct Mrs. Spencer that she is totally responsible for the children while they are in her home."

Unforgiving as Idalynn was toward Michael, she wanted to appeal this direction of the court. Lulu Lee advised her daughter, "Idalynn accept all of this as a new beginning for all of us. At least you are free from Michael." Idalynn was calmed with the feeling that just maybe, she, her mother and the children, were a little closer to reaching Lexington.

All too soon, Idalynn's positive feelings turned to anger when she was reminded that the court had granted Michael the right to decide if, or when, the children could leave the state of Wisconsin. Michael could also decide the length of time that the children could remain out of the state. Idalynn resented these restrictions. Lulu Lee insisted to Idalynn, that for the moment, she should remain silent.

Michael's leaving the family home greatly impacted the children's lives. With the divorce, they had lost a cherished playmate. He had always been the one to suggest fun things to do, whether it was hiking, swimming or drinking malted milks together at the corner drug store. That period of happiness had disappeared.

Now, Lulu Lee, the former Lexington most admired society matron, and Idalynn, the former Lexington debutante, were both divorced and facing a future of uncertainty. Foremost on Lulu Lee's mind now, was the welfare of three adorable little girls, her grandbabies.

A Changed Life for All

It was the 1940's. Values were changing. Things were changing in Michael's life. The divorce from his wife with all of its ramifications, along with the separation from his children, made him realize that he was not truly a successful man in life. He had failed his own family by not being a better take-charge husband and father. He wondered if it was too late to change the grave misfortunes that had befallen all of them.

Michael decided to leave the pursuit of criminals to the younger man—something that Idalynn had always begged him to do. It was time to settle down in one locale, in a home which he could be proud. He submitted his resignation to J. Edgar Hoover, left the Chicago area, and moved to Indiana, where he accepted a position of a court judge. He decided to let someone else chase down the criminals. He would judge them when they arrived in his court.

With Michael moving to Indiana, the courts deemed the children must either stay in school in the state of Wisconsin where they would be under jurisdiction of the court or move to the state of Indiana, under the custodial care of their father. Remaining in Wisconsin was the only logical choice that Lulu Lee and Idalynn could make. Michael could only hope that one day the children would want to come to him, at least for short visits.

The divorce proved exceptionally difficult for the children; in the many years to come, they would only see their father, once a year—some years, not at all. The children felt underprivileged, not in the sense of money, but being from a divorced family. They were alienated from their friends. It meant not being invited to parties, and even being denied the friendship of some of their playmates.

Lulu Lee, Idalynn and the children's lives were about to make still another change. Not wanting to remain in a large metropolitan city such as Milwaukee, they decided to move further north in the state, to a town with a population of 20,000, called Fond du Lac.

Fond du Lac was a lovely town on Lake Winnebago. It was Lulu Lee's plan to open a gracious rooming house, with Southern hospitality. It was the only way that Lulu Lee knew how to maintain a good life for all of them. She was most anxious and confident to try her idea.

Not only was moving day an exciting day for the children, but also for Lulu Lee and Idalynn. They looked upon the move to Fond du Lac as a positive action in their lives. Most importantly, they were distancing themselves from the Milwaukee memories of the mental institution, as well as the divorce and, of course, Michael's mother. Realistically, all would become memories that would never be forgotten. Wanting respect, they hoped to meet new people, who would accept them—especially the children.

Lulu Lee and the children were very excited when they saw the home that Idalynn had chosen for the family to rent. It was a large Victorian house, with twelve rooms and front and back staircases. On the outside, a large-wrap around front porch added a final touch of elegance to the home. The children especially loved the large side yard with its many shaded elm trees, where they would be able to play their games.

As the movers carried the furniture into the house, there were painters working on the outside, painting the house an olive green color. The interior of the home had just been freshly painted as well. The home on 125 Third Street had beautiful curb appeal.

One of the painters happened to tell Lulu Lee that a man had recently been murdered in the house. It was said that he had been shot under the crystal chandelier in the front hall and, subsequently, bled to death. The murder was a shocking event in Fond du Lac and had caused much notoriety. Already, people were wondering what type of people would want to inhabit a house where such a horrible crime had occurred, so recently!

Newspaper and on-the-spot radio reporters were at the house, wanting to interview Lulu Lee or Idalynn about their plans to once again make this home a desirable place in which to live. Lulu Lee silently wondered if anyone would want to patronize such a home under the circumstances, with all the negative publicity. Perhaps this was another wrong move in their lives.

In spite of all of the unfavorable talk, a lovely existence was created in this home. With the money coming in from several boarders, as well as the alimony checks from Charles and Michael, a very pleasant lifestyle was afforded. The Chamber of Commerce listed this home "top of the list" for anyone needing an interim place in which to live.

Almost immediately, it became necessary to create a waiting list of names for those who wished to preside even temporarily, in these lovely surroundings. Lulu Lee and Idalynn were looked upon very favorably, and Fond du Lac opened its arms to these two gracious women, who bore all the marks of Southern ladies offering a "Southern hospitality" home.

In the midst of World War II, it was considered patriotic to list your home with the USO (United Service Organization), should you wish to invite a soldier to enjoy Sunday dinner in your home. It was noted in the town newspaper, that Idalynn and Lulu Lee were among the first to partake of opening their home for such a purpose. The town newspaper was quick to point out the "warm welcome to a soldier" in this very lovely place.

The olive green home on Third Street was furnished with Chippendale furniture. A maroon striped, satin couch; a Spinet piano with a white leather bench; Austrian China and the finest lamps and accessories were just some of the

touches depicting elegance. Once again, Mulberry was created, emanating a flavor from the past. The children were
fashionably dressed, and the family facade appeared to
be that of privilege. For a while, a very special home had
been established.

Lee was enrolled at St. Mary's Springs Academy, a private
school, just outside of town. She enjoyed being in school
plays and had several close friends. She rode to school on
the private academy school bus. Her younger sisters attended St. Joseph's Catholic School on Second Street, in the
heart of town.

Fond du Lac was becoming a special place in the children's hearts. In winter, they ice skated on the various city
ponds, with bonfires and shanties with pot bellied stoves
to warm themselves. Sleigh rides were a favorite thing to
do. Even walking to school in the deep snow, jumping from
snow bank to snow bank was delightful for the children. At
times, the ice on the river jammed under the bridges just
west of Main Street. This was mesmerizing to the children
at times, causing them to be late for school.

In summer the gazebo at Lakeside Park was where the
weekly band concerts were held, weather permitting. Pete
Mingles was a favorite swimming beach. If one chose, they
also had the choice of swimming at the very huge pool at
Taylor Park on Forest Avenue. McKnight's Drugstore was
a favorite place for the young teenagers to "hang out," while
Plank's Drugstore at Third and Main was noted for giving a

free pint of ice cream if you got a green gum ball out of the gum machine. These were unforgettable memories.

Fond du Lac would also hold the best and the worst of all of their memories. The children were living in the innocent years of their lives, yet they would have to grow up faster then most children, especially with the events that were on the horizon.

After living in Fond du Lac for two years, Idalynn became very restless. Once again, she was unable to find friendships. Trying to ignore the labels of "divorced women," placed upon them, Lulu Lee and Idalynn continued to hold their heads high, and tried to be a part of the community. It was difficult to do so during the 1940's, as women's reputations were tainted when that label was associated with them.

Consequently, Idalynn frequented various taverns, craving friendships and attention that until now had eluded her. She used what money she had to buy drinks for people she hardly knew. This was a practice that Idalynn could ill afford. When Lulu Lee challenged her on these practices, Idalynn insisted that she be allowed to live her life, on her own terms.

Not known to Lulu Lee, Idalynn fell behind with the rent payments. Shockingly, when Idalynn became embroiled in a dispute with the landlady, an eviction notice was served to the women. Unable to offer monies for past due rental payments, Idalynn and Lulu Lee were forced to move, leaving behind the lovely home that Lulu Lee had established. Lulu Lee was heartsick!

Idalynn found another lovely home, located in Oskosh, just thirty miles north of Fond du Lac, and across Lake Winnebago. Lulu Lee and Idalynn were not aware that the former landlady in Fond du Lac was following the moving truck to their new home. She met with the new landlady and convinced her that Idalynn and Lulu Lee were not suitable to be tenants, preventing the women and the children from moving into their new home.

With no other option, the moving van took their furniture to a storage warehouse, the family never realizing that they would not ever see their furniture and precious possessions again. Their treasures emulating Mulberry would be gone forever. From this point on, their lives once again, spiraled downward—only faster than ever before.

One would always wonder if the former landlady in Fond du Lac knew that she had assisted in destroying a large part of this family's lives. There would be so many years of strife and suffering as a result of her actions.

Lulu Lee made the decision that they needed to return to Fond du Lac, where there were at least familiar surroundings. In doing so, the five of them moved into one room at the downtown Retlaw Hotel for several weeks to think things through and evaluate their finances. Eating all of their meals in restaurants, as well as sending their clothes to be washed at the laundry, was taking a drastic toll on their income.

With hotel expenses escalating, they decided to move into a rooming house, not at all like the home that they had so recently provided for the town. It was so emotionally painful to walk past the olive green house that had once been their beautiful residence. Seeing a new family sitting on their screened in porch was heart wrenching—while Lulu Lee, Idalynn, and the three children, were living in one room.

Trying to cut back on expenses, Lulu Lee asked the lady running the boarding house, if she could assist her with cooking and cleaning for her boarders—anything to help their financial predicament. While Lulu Lee was busily assisting their landlady, or watching over the children at play in the yard, Idalynn was upstairs in their room reading, and seemingly not giving a thought to their dire circumstances.

Lulu Lee could not help but think back to what the psychiatrist at the State Hospital in Waupon had said about "lack of accountability" regarding Idalynn. It was all true.

When Lulu Lee tried to impress upon Idalynn how bad things were, Idalynn insisted that she had a plan to make things right. When Idalynn could not come up with a plan, Lulu Lee recognized that once again, Idalynn was delusional and had regressed to her world of fantasy. After several weeks, they were asked to leave for not being able to contribute sufficient monies to pay the rent.

Moving to another boarding home across town, where they hoped they would not be known to have come from the previous one, they told the owners that they were in transit, awaiting their furniture to be delivered from another part of the country. Lulu Lee and Idalynn, wearing their dresses with white lace collars and pearls, appeared to be very pleasant and trusting ladies. No one would suspect that they and the children were destitute and were in the process of shunting from one boarding house to the next one.

———

The Christmas holidays were spent in one room, where they had an eighteen-inch imitation Christmas tree for the children. Everything was so diverse from the other "Norman Rockwell" Christmas Holidays, they had known in the past. Their address was, "General Delivery."

With five of them living in one room and sleeping in two beds at the tourist home Lulu Lee had no other options but to write to Charles to tell him of their plight.

Dear Charlie,

It is with much embarrassment that I am writing to you to ask you for financial assistance. Idalynn and I, and the grandchildren, are in dire need of your concern for us. I have hesitated in writing this letter to ask you for assistance, as circumstances are just too complex to try to explain it all, but I have no other choice. If you could find it in your heart, please send us five hundred dollars to help us live a decent life. I promise to explain all this to you, one day.

Affectionately,

Lulu Lee

Charles responded immediately:

Dear Lulu Lee,

Enclosed is a check in the amount you requested. Are you certain that this is all you need? Please know that you never have to explain anything to me.

Charlie

Charles' check was to afford Lulu Lee the ability to re-trieve their furniture from storage so Lulu Lee could re-establish a home. With back rents owed, eating in restaurants and needing to purchase clothes for the children to wear to school, there still was not sufficient money to pay the storage bill. They were no further ahead.

Within a short time, a second request to Charles for money was made, and Charles sent several hundred dollars again. Lulu Lee accepted the previous mismanagement of monies as her own doings, rather than expose Idalynn to her father. Since Charles so adored his daughter, Lulu Lee did not want to destroy the vision that he had of her.

Not feeling well, Lulu Lee entrusted the money to Idalynn to go down town to send a money order to pay the storage bill in Oshkosh. In the meantime, when her health permitted, Lulu Lee spent time looking for another suitable house to re-establish a home. Although Idalynn told her mother that she had sent the money owed to the storage company, she had not. Again, in her own fashion, Idalynn had spent the money at the taverns she had frequented in the past. It was important to Idalynn to keep up appearances, before the people she thought were her friends.

Lulu Lee was shocked when she received a notice from the warehouse in Oshkosh that payment in arrears had been made with the monies acquired at the auction of the Spencer furniture. Lulu Lee had never been made aware that the storage company had given them notice that their furniture was to be sold at auction by a designated date. Idalynn had intercepted that letter at the post office.

When Lulu Lee realized that they had lost everything, for the first time ever Lulu Lee slapped Idalynn across the face! Lulu Lee's relationship with her daughter had become a sweeping saga of mistrust.

Just when Lulu Lee and the children were starting to think of the possibilities of a home of their own, they had to come to the realization that these were only dreams.

Mulberry was no longer in reach. Three years had gone by since they had moved from their lovely Victorian home in Fond du Lac. Now, they were living in less than adequate conditions.

During the past three years, the only contact that Michael had with his children was through the General Delivery mail address. He was not certain as to where they actually lived, and there was no telephone number afforded to him. He was very concerned, as he knew that they were changing residences frequently by virtue of the cards that the children had sent to him on various occasions. Idalynn countered by saying he was a trained investigator, and that he could have found them, if he had wanted to do so. Michael accepted that retort as valid. He too, had failed the children.

Lulu Lee finally had to admit to herself, that not only was Idalynn an irresponsible person, living in a make believe world and accepting no blame; but that Idalynn did need mental help. Looking back, she realized that she could not be certain that she nor Charles had ever permitted Idalynn to grow emotionally, or to be a responsible person.

Charles had always said to his family that rules were for other people. It was apparent that Idalynn remembered those early unforgettable words, and believed him. She never chose to play by the rules. Adding to the destruction of Idalynn, was the fact that she was the only child born to any of the Spencer brothers and their families, and they literally waited for this child to run to them for anything that she desired. Lulu Lee finally had to admit to herself that her daughter was a beautiful woman with an extremely disturbing mind.

Lulu Lee had spent her lifetime covering for Idalynn, in every way that she knew how. In reality, she knew that she had four children to tend. She knew she had to take complete control over Idalynn. Lulu Lee felt helpless. At times, she felt it was hopeless as well.

In all that had transpired, Idalynn was a good mother in many ways—the best that she knew how to be. She played games and paper dolls with the children, taught them songs to sing, and helped them all to learn to read before entering kindergarten. Idalynn was caring and loving. She just never acquired the ability to mature. Essentially, Idalynn was the children's playmate.

Lulu Lee could no longer stand their living conditions and all the uncertainty that went with it. With a sense of urgency, and the swallowing of any pride that she might have had, Lulu Lee, made a call to her sister Jennie, in Horse Cave, to ask for advice and financial assistance. Lulu Lee only wished that she had done this before, not letting pride stand in the way.

"Jennie? It's Lulu Lee!"

Jennie said, "Lulu Lee, where are you? Where have you been? We have been worried sick over all of you!"

Jennie was thrilled to finally hear from her baby sister. Jennie had been trying for many months to contact Lulu

Lee, but her letters had always been returned—"No Longer At This Address," "No Forwarding Address."

"Oh, Jennie, it's such a long story. So sad! So unbelievable! I don't know how I allowed us to get into the situation that I find us in."

Listening to her sister tell her all that had happened, Jennie wired money to them immediately, encouraging all of them to come home to Lexington where she and her husband were moving within a few days. Due to the illness of Jennie's husband, Jennie decided that they needed to be closer to larger medical facilities.

Jennie told Lulu Lee, "Mulberry is up for sale and any proceeds from the sale of the estate will certainly belong to all of the siblings." Jennie insisted that they would all stay with her until they could find suitable lodging. Jennie continued, "Lulu Lee, I just wish that you had contacted me sooner. You all need to be with relatives who care about you." These were wonderful words for Lulu Lee to hear! Lulu Lee took a deep breath and tried to hold back the tears.

Idalynn contacted Michael immediately, to advise him that it was important for her and the children to move back to Lexington to be closer to Mama's sister, as her mother, Lulu Lee was not in good health. She implored Michael to seek legal permission, allowing her to change their residency as soon as possible.

Michael saw no reason as to why they should not move to Lexington; in fact, this move, would put the children in closer proximity to him in Indiana. It only took one phone call by Michael to the judge. The courts granted the request.

Lulu Lee, Idalynn, and the children were excited beyond words. After so many years of dreaming of journeying home to Lexington, they would now be going in the right direction, toward having a home of their own. What they didn't know was, this happiness would never materialize.

Heartbreak

Having lived a nomadic-type lifestyle for such a long time, Lulu Lee had not been under proper medical attention. She had continually ignored the symptoms of being seriously ill. After being admitted to the hospital in Fond du Lac for tests, the doctor said, "Mrs. Spencer, I am so dreadfully sorry to inform you that you have an advanced stage of ovarian cancer." He sadly told her that she had less than six months to live.

Although Lulu Lee knew she was at the end of her own life, she still worried about those she would leave behind. Telling Idalynn and Jennie would be extremely difficult for her.

"Idalynn Dear, I must tell you what the doctor has told me. I have ovarian cancer and have just a short time to be with you. I have been given a diagnosis that is fatal. We must talk about yours, and the children's, future. We have much preparation in which to do."

While Idalynn sobbed, Lulu Lee was very silent. She knew she had to reach Michael in order to make plans.

Idalynn frantically called her father to tell him her mother was in the hospital facing a terminal illness.

Charles called Lulu Lee at the hospital, to tell her how dreadful he felt with the thought of her being so ill. He said, "Lulu Lee, I wish that I were there with you. Whatever you need or want, just call me. I have arranged for all of your medical bills to be directed to me. Call me anytime for anything. You will constantly be on my mind."

Lulu Lee wrote to Michael in Indiana, telling him of her illness. She asked him to come to Fond du Lac as soon as possible, under the pretense of visiting the children. She said she needed to discuss important matters with him. She urged him not to wait too long.

With Michael's immediate arrival in Fond du Lac, he went to the hospital where Lulu Lee was undergoing radiation treatments. She was very ill and experiencing great pain, but she still needed to speak with Michael. She needed assurances from him.

Lulu Lee begged Michael to be there for the children, as well as for Idalynn, when the time came should she die. Lulu Lee asked over and over, "What will become of my grandbabies?" Lulu Lee said, "Michael, promise me that you will not let the children fall back to the life from which they have just been rescued. Promise me that!"

Michael gave her his oath. Michael said, "Mother Spencer, You are not to worry about the children. I give you my oath. I will take care of everyone."

When Idalynn saw Michael in Fond du Lac, she wanted to hate him, but instead, she slumped into his arms and cried. She simply did not know where to turn. Idalynn was distraught beyond words over her mother's grave illness. The thought of losing Mama, who was always there to pick up the pieces for her during her entire life, was more than Idalynn could bear. Although Michael was legally no longer a part of her life, Idalynn knew she needed him to help her get through all this. For the first time in her life, Idalynn was facing having to stand on her own, and be a responsible person. Idalynn realized that she didn't know how to do that.

Two weeks later, not expecting her mother's imminent death, Idalynn left town for the weekend to visit some friends. Idalynn had been spending the days and nights sitting by Mama's bedside. The doctor advised her to take a break, and assured her that Lulu Lee would be in good hands. It was while Idalynn was out of town that Lulu Lee, took a sudden unexpected turn for the worst, and slipped into a coma.

The children prayed for a miracle so that their Mama would not have to leave them, but that was not to be. The ravages of the fast growing cancer had finally conquered her.

The three grandchildren were at their Mama's bedside, when she died. Moments before her death, Lulu Lee awakened from her coma, turned to the children and said, "Babies, now don't you cry." It was New Year's Eve, 1947. Mama was in the past!

The children called their father in Indiana, crying, telling them that Mama had died that very evening. They innocently told him that their mother was not at home. When Michael inquired as to where she was, they responded that they did not know. Lee, who was seventeen years old, had been left in charge of her two younger sisters. Michael responded by saying, he would start out driving to Fond du Lac and would be there in a few hours. In the meantime, Michael called Charles in Tennessee to advise him of Lulu Lee's passing. He encouraged Charles to meet him in Fond du Lac as soon as possible.

Charles and Michael were in Fond du Lac before Idalynn arrived home the next day. Charles met his three grandchildren for the first time. One thing stood out in the children's minds. As they were introduced to their grandfather, he did not make any overtures to them. It was as though they were strangers to him. Charles appeared to be heartless and indifferent. It was apparent that whatever he did for all of them, was done out of his love and concern for his former wife, Lulu Lee. Michael could not understand Charles' coldness. Michael could not help but notice that Idalynn had done a superior job in teaching the children perfect manners, and he was very proud of them. How could Charles not notice this—or love them?

Charles took it upon himself to make all the funeral arrangements for Lulu Lee. Out of his anger toward Idalynn, he planned the funeral whether Idalynn would make it home or not. Not known to Idalynn, when she arrived home, it was the designated day for her Mama's funeral. As Idalynn stepped off the train, nothing could have prepared her to meet Michael or the children or her enraged father—enraged for not being with her mother, on her deathbed.

Idalynn said, "Michael, Daddy, what are you doing here? How is Mama?"

The notoriously short-tempered Charles yelled at Idalynn, "You left your mother's death bedside. She died without you. You are such a disappointment to me. You are no daughter of mine!"

Being greeted with the words that her mother had died, Idalynn paled, trembled and nearly collapsed. Michael assisted her to a bench, while the children, crying along with her, stroked and hugged her.

Idalynn said, "Oh Michael, how can I go on without Mama? I want the past back! I cannot bear the present!"

Charles, not caring whether Idalynn was near collapse or not, continued to yell at her. "I disowned you before, and I plan to disown you again! You, nor anyone who reminds me of you, will have a future of any inheritance from me!" Following that threat, he wired his attorney later that day of his intentions. Michael held his resentment of Charles' behavior quietly inside of him.

But Lee, Emily and Suzanne were visibly angry. Lulu Lee had always instilled great confidences in her grandchildren. They had been taught that they were just as good as anyone else, and whatever they had to say, deserved to be heard. Their grandmother had given the children stability and security. She had always loved them and they knew it. With their grandfather's abrasive tone to their mother, they bristled and stood up to him in defiance. They intended to be heard.

Lee turned and shouted at her grandfather. "Go away! We don't want you here. We don't know you and you can't boss our family." Not realizing the consequences of her action toward her grandfather, Lee turned to her father and said, "Daddy, don't let him yell at Mother. Please make him go away."

Michael hugged the children close to him and said, "Let's go, family. We must say our good byes to Mama."

Lulu Lee's death wasn't something that the three grandchildren would ever "get over;" rather, it was a deep sorrow that would simply become a part of their lives. The void created, due to her absence in their lives, would never be completely filled again.

Michael tried to reassure the children by telling them their pain of missing Mama would always enable them to remember her. Michael said, "Children, in order to live now, we must let go of the past. We must also help your mother to get through this."

Within four or five days of Michael's arrival in town, he reluctantly had to make arrangements for the children to be given to his custody. It was the law that had been directed at the time of the divorce by the courts. Michael had permitted the children to remain in Idalynn's home, provided they were under the supervision and care of Lulu Lee Spencer. Now that Lulu Lee was no longer with them, the courts decreed that the children legally had to be with their father. He was to take the girls, to live with him in Indiana.

Michael did not want to add to Idalynn's grief by telling her that her own mother had begged him to take care of the children after her death, so Michael played the part of the villain. It was the only option that he felt he had; otherwise, the children were to be put in foster care. Michael would never have allowed that; nor would he want Idalynn to suffer that humiliation.

Strange as it would seem, there was still a part of Michael that worried and cared about Idalynn. Michael had made a promise to Lulu Lee that he would take care of everyone, and out of his respect and love for her, as well as feeling honor-bound, he meant to keep his word. Michael would never allow himself to forget that his mother-in-law had been a stabilizing force for him and his children when they all needed her.

Although Lulu Lee had only lived in Fond du Lac less than three years before her death, her funeral was well attended. The ladies who offered "southern hospitality" had not been forgotten. The children and their mother sat on the front row at the funeral parlor while Michael and Charles sat directly behind them.

As the children sat quietly, trying to smother the sounds of their own crying with their handkerchiefs, their tears flowed abundantly. Idalynn was inconsolable. She knew that the loss of her mother meant a loss of herself. She simply could not bear the thought of life without her. She was emotionally chained to a past that included her mother.

The family had endured many tragic obstacles together, and now losing this warm and loving woman was an unimagined horror in their lives. Michael was aware that with the loss of this wonderful person, the children were now deprived of a kind, and devoted grandmother. He only hoped that his promise to his mother-in-law had brought her some peace and made dying a little easier.

The organ started to play, *Ave Maria*, one of Lulu Lee's favorite songs. Charles recognized the music as the music that had been played at their wedding, and tears filled his eyes. He was shaken and trying his best to be in control of his emotions. He started to sob one moment, and the next moment, he was silent. Charles appeared to lean toward Michael, but then his body slumped forward.

Michael jumped to his feet to help Charles, while calling for assistance. The doctor who had attended Lulu Lee in life, was present among the mourners. He rushed to Charles' side.

The doctor surmised Charles had suffered a heart attack and administered to him in the best way that he could for the moment. With an ambulance on the way, the funeral ceremony was delayed, while all present silently prayed.

Idalynn could not accept what was happening. Becoming hysterical, she rushed to Michael's side and screamed, "Michael, don't let this be happening! Help him! Help him!" Then Idalynn collapsed.

The children withdrew to the side of the room. Not only were they crying for their grandmother, now they were also crying about their mother. None of the girls acknowledged their grandfather illness. After all, they had only just met him.

Michael assumed the position as head of the family, and took matters into his own hands. While others attended Idalynn, Michael rode in the ambulance with the doctor and Charles, who had by now regained consciousness. Charles insisted, "I just fainted due to the heavy aroma of flowers and close air. I insist that you take me back to the funeral where I can bid my last farewell to a very dear lady from my past."

Against the doctor's wishes, the ambulance turned around to return to the funeral services and burial of the young girl whom he had fallen so completely in love so many years ago. Immediately following the funeral services, without spending time to bid his farewells to anyone, Charles Spencer left to return to Tennessee. Michael had been left the responsibility to see that Lulu Lee's body was to be shipped to Lexington for burial in the Spencer family designated plots —as per Charles' instructions.

Along with tremendous grief over the loss of her mother, and watching her father's collapse, and knowing that she was not able to approach him to offer comfort, Idalynn too suffered a complete nervous breakdown. She was hospitalized—perhaps from heartbreak, or guilt, or even fear of what would become of all of them now. She thought to herself, "Only days earlier, Mama had been with us, and we were a family. Now we are alone." A door to the past had closed. Idalynn could not bear the present.

Lulu Lee had been a compassionate and caring person. She was truthful and trustworthy and had given up enhancing her own life to greater heights, so her daughter and grandchildren would know love, and feel secure. Now, Lulu Lee was no longer with them and Idalynn would also need to be separated from her family, for an indefinite period of time.

Michael spoke to Idalynn in endearing terms. "Please don't concern yourself about anything other than your own health. I will take the children back to Indiana to enroll them in school. You need only to tell me when you are ready for the girls to return." He thought to himself that he would cross that legality when and if the time came.

The children learned at this point of their lives, that life could not go backwards. It could either stand still, or move forward. Michael felt the children would be moving forward in their lives, by moving to Indiana. The children wanted to stand still.

The night before they were to leave, the three girls cried themselves to sleep. The girls did not want to live with their father, to go back to an unknown area, to start life anew, again. They also did not want to leave their mother. They knew she needed them.

The girls were very sad the next day, when it was time to say good-bye to their mother at the hospital. Even though their father assured the girls that they would be coming back to see her whenever there was any type of school vacations, they were already missing her. Idalynn was not only sad, but she was frightened as she saw her children walk out of her hospital room with their father. She could not help but think that she would never again regain what she had just lost. Now she was truly alone.

As Idalynn sat in her hospital room, there was so many questions running through her mind. She wondered how long she would have to be in the hospital? She wondered how the girls would manage living with their father? She wondered what the future would be for any of them.

While the girls were driving back to Indiana with their father, it was difficult for them to hold back their tears. Since it had been the Christmas holidays from school, when their grandmother had died, they had not had the opportunity to say good-bye to their friends. Everything had happened so quickly.

Although the move to Indiana was a life-saving move for the children, it was still a difficult move, especially for

Lee, who only had one high school semester to complete. Now she would need to finish her senior year, in a strange city, with new classmates, leaving her previous high school friends behind. In many ways, the move to Indiana represented the end of a dependent childhood for the girls. From this point on, they would no longer be allowed to be children.

———————

Upon returning home to Tennessee, Charles became bedridden with heart problems. Weeks later he called Michael on the telephone. Charles said, "Michael, I know that my time for living is very limited. I have been very depressed just recalling my earlier life of how I behaved, as well as not being closer to the grandchildren so that I might have known them. I am heartbroken just thinking about actions toward my only daughter during her mother's funeral. I cannot tell you how terrible I feel for the way I behaved in front of Lulu Lee's and my grandchildren. Not only was that the first time that I had ever seen them, it was most assuredly my last time to be with them. I must contact my attorney later today to rescind my instructions of omitting Idalynn and the children from my will. I only hope that one day they will forgive me. I will also write to Idalynn, to tell her that in spite of everything, I do love her very much. Hopefully she will realize that matters pertaining to the children are in her best interest. Having said that, Michael, I want you to know that I am calmed that the children are with you." Not feeling well enough to write the letter to his daughter, Charles delayed doing it until the next day. During the night, Charles suffered another heart attack and died—six months after Lulu Lee had died.

Those who knew Charles well, felt that in the last few weeks of his life, he had been a sad and distraught man. Many of Lulu Lee's friends commented that more than likely, Charles had died of a broken heart, knowing that Lulu Lee was no longer alive. Charles' present wife did not let Michael, Idalynn or the children know of Charles' death until after the funeral and burial.

Alone

Due to Idalynn's fragile state, Michael advised Charles' attorney that he was taking care of Idalynn's legal affairs. He said he wanted to be informed of the contents of Charles' will and be sent a copy of such. Michael also requested that all legal matters were to be sent to his office, as Idalynn Brooks was not to be contacted for anything.

Having witnessed Charles' tirade at the railroad station, Michael was not surprised to find out that neither Idalynn's or the children's names were mentioned as heirs to any part of his vast fortune. Unfortunately for Idalynn and the children, Charles Spencer had waited too long to rethink his anger toward his daughter and grandchildren.

Michael kept in close contact with Idalynn during her hospitalization, making certain the children called their mother every week, and wrote to her often—always enclosing a check, supposedly from her father, which of course, was provided by Michael. He informed Idalynn that he had been put in charge of hers and the children's inheritance from her father. All of her hospital bills were to be sent directly to him, and whenever she left the hospital, she was to send all her personal bills to him as well. Idalynn was relieved to know that her father had loved her, and the children, in spite of all that had taken place.

Michael realized that the move to Indiana was a big adjustment and upheaval for the children. Trying to compensate for this, he was very generous to them when it came to their wanting or needing anything. He was trying to do his best.

Ironically, the people who lived in the city where Michael lived were astonished when "the Judge" showed up with three teenage daughters. Many eligible women, who sought out the attention of this handsome and engaging man, were not aware that Michael had ever been married. He was that sort of private person.

While Idalynn was under the care of a psychiatrist, she was informed that tests performed showed that she had a condition, referred to as a chemical imbalance. The doctor advised her that as a result, any inconsequential thing could cause her to feel sad and morose, perhaps even triggering her mind to simulate irresponsible actions.

When Idalynn asked the doctor if this was something that suggested she needed to have a lengthy hospitalization, the doctor assured her that no amount of internment would help her condition. With proper medication over a period of time, a state of normalcy possibly could be restored to her, offering her a productive life ahead.

The doctor advised her that for her to successfully live in the present, she would need to let go of the past.

Days later, when Idalynn was released from the hospital, she returned to the little home, which she, her mother and children had shared for a short time. She wrote very sad letters to the children, saying she was emotionally drained and felt as though she were merely existing. She alluded to the fact that she could not bear her present life.

Idalynn was reminded of the doctor's words that it was normal to feel useless or sad, as she was in a long and slow recovery. The doctor had said, "Idalynn, emotional pain is the same as physical pain. Call it what you wish, the name doesn't matter as long as you recognize it."

Idalynn talked on the telephone with her aunt frequently. Jennie was elderly and for the most part, housebound. Idalynn hesitated to bother Jennie with mentioning any of her own problems; they just enjoyed family closeness. By all accounts, now, she definitely needed someone.

But Idalynn had always needed "someone" during her entire life. In her case, it had been Mama. Idalynn recognized that she had been an emotional invalid and lived only within her mother's carefully invented world for her. Now she had to live in the moment.

Idalynn decided to set plans into motion and move to Lexington immediately. She planned to sell her furniture and pack the rest. After all, Mama was already there and moving to Lexington had always been the big plan.

Six months later, Michael was astounded when the children received a letter from their mother, telling them of her plans to remarry. The man she intended to marry was a land developer from Atlanta, Georgia. She had met him when she was volunteering for a charity ball, looking for sponsors, as her own father had done many years ago. More accurately, Idalynn recognized that she was desperate for someone, with whom to share her life.

The man in her life, at the moment, was Gregory Patterson. He possessed all the qualifications that she thought necessary for the life she wanted to lead. She compared him to her father. Not only was he a successful businessman, he was a charming conversationalist. Most importantly, he was a Southerner. While Michael was quite surprised, he did realize that he would have to accept the fact that Idalynn wanted to be married, just not to him.

Idalynn's usual air of presumptiveness afforded her to move about in Lexington's lofty social circles. With an escort of outstanding credentials, she knew she would be able to mingle with the best. The dark side of Idalynn was she was not always able to show deference to people who were in opposition to her thinking, opinion, or judgment. At times, people chose to avoid her, rather than be in conflict with her. She was not one to accept any responsibility, for any consequence. Again, friendships withdrew from her.

When Gregory mentioned their moving to Atlanta after they were married, Idalynn's doubts began to surface. She wasn't certain that she wanted to be with him at all. Idalynn commented, "But Gregory, Lexington is my home. My mother is buried here. I could never leave the city of my roots." Gregory commented, "Surely we can work through all this. Let's discuss it in detail when I return from an Atlanta."

While Gregory was driving to Atlanta, a semi-truck blew a tire and spun the wheel across the median, hitting Gregory's windshield. Gregory lost control of his car, sending it down an embankment into a ravine. He was killed instantly.

Idalynn was in a state of shock. She was facing extreme sadness once again in her life. While she appeared to others as charming, enchanting and witty, she was ultimately a tragic person. Life presented a poignant portrait of a woman destined to loneliness.

Idalynn told her daughters about Gregory's accident and demise. Michael, when he heard about the situation, called and invited her to Indiana to visit with the children. Wanting to go where she knew people cared about her, Idalynn accepted.

Idalynn came to town, merely as a mother visiting her children, but the town's people looked upon her as the

"Judge's wife." She was the subject on everyone's tongue. Not only was she the mysterious woman in the Judge's past life, she was a very lovely and gracious woman. So many people were eager to cross paths with her. Many social invitations were extended; but Idalynn declined all of them.

Michael was pleased to have Idalynn back with the children and the children loved every minute of it. They wanted to care for her and hear her laugh again. In the back of Michael's mind was the illusive hope, that one day, they would all be a family again.

———————

Idalynn made frequent visits to Indiana to be with the children. She so enjoyed assisting the girls with choosing their gowns for their various dances. It was even more fun to assist them in dressing, and later, meeting their beaus. She remembered Mama playing this same role with her.

Ironically on one visit, Idalynn, once again met up with Michael's former boss, Eliot Ness while he too was visiting Michael. As the three of them conversed about their pasts, Idalynn remembered how she had detested the times when Mr. Ness had come to their home in Chicago to discuss modes of operation during those Al Capone days. Conversely, now each of them were at a different point in their lives and she was happy and relaxed to be a part of such a social reunion.

Michael never spoke to anyone of when Eliot planned to visit with him and insisted to the girls that they too had to maintain a decorm of silence about Mr. Ness' planned visits. No one in town ever knew when Eliot Ness arrived or departed from their small Indiana town. Idalynn well understood Mr. Ness' feelings about his visits as she too enjoyed her visits more when she could slip in and out of town inconspicuously.

It was during one visit to Indiana that Idalynn commented to the girls that the Colonial home in Lexington, which had belonged to her mother and father on Versailles Parkway, was up for sale. Idalynn commented that it was still such a beautiful and magnificent home. She happily talked to the children about all the wonderful memories that she and her family, and their father for that matter, had experienced in the house. She mentioned to them, that it was that home where she and their father had been married.

Michael jumped to his feet and said, "Idalynn, I'd like to drive to Lexington to see that house again. Just to walk through it would be wonderful! Why don't we go see the house, just for old time's sake? It would be wonderful to show the girls this grand home that played such an important part in our lives."

With the girls gleefully wanting to see this home that they had heard so much about, Idalynn agreed. After all that had transpired in their lives together, Idalynn finally felt comfortable, just being with Michael.

Walking through her home from the past was very emotional for Idalynn. She recalled when she and Michael had come home from Chicago to visit her parents, and there, at the dining room table, Michael had proudly told all of them of the offer afforded to him to be an Ambassador to Nicaragua. Thinking back about that evening, Idalynn was embarrassed as to how she had reacted. Michael had possessed abilities that would have taken him far in the political world, had she not ruined that for him.

Michael preferred to remember the first time that he came to call upon Idalynn, how he thought the home and Idalynn's parents were all so gracious. He thought it was a perfect setting. Hearing all this, Idalynn's eyes sparkled; then they teared.

The house held so many ghosts from the past. As they strolled through the house Idalynn could feel her mother's presence in every room and she felt as though she were communing with her mother; especially remembering her mother's beautiful portrait hanging above the fireplace mantel. She did notice that the house had weathered the years, beautifully. It was comforting to presume that all who had spent time in this house had obviously loved it and had maintained it well. It all seemed so surreal.

Just before walking out of the magnificent front hall, Michael quietly suggested, out of the girl's hearing, "Idalynn, I'm tempted to put a bid in for this house. It could be an investment for the girls, and in the meantime, you could live in it!" Although, it seemed more like happy talk, Idalynn was enjoying the moment.

———————

Michael bought the house, and Idalynn was ecstatic the day she moved into the home that had belonged to her parents. Idalynn tried to place her own furniture much in the fashion which her mother had done. The marble fireplace, where she and Michael had been married, was still as beautiful as it had been on her wedding day. To put the finishing touch to the move to this lovely home, Michael surprised her with a kick plate on the front door inscribed, "Mulberry."

Tears came to her eyes when she looked at the window where her mother's favorite chair had been placed. She remembered her Bulldog, Pat Bailey, had perched on that chair, to look out over the expansive veranda. It was as though for a moment she could hear Mama reprimanding the dog for being on the chair. A smile came to Idalynn's face as she remembered how many times Pat Bailey had knocked ice cream cones out of children's hands as they passed the house. Her mother had had to keep a collection of nickels to give to the children so they could replace their cones—as Pat Bailey enjoyed theirs. It almost seemed that her previous lifetime was resurrecting itself. She could actually feel the love that had existed in this lovely home.

Months passed. Idalynn at last was at peace with herself. She thought to herself that Mama would have been proud of her. She also felt that Michael and she had reached a plateau where they had finally become good friends.

Whenever she had tried to speak with Michael, regarding her past feelings and behavior, Michael would stop her with his comment, "Idalynn, we both meant well. It is not necessary that we ever bring up our turbulent past again."

Even though the old adage, "Life cannot go backwards.....," she felt as though she had gone backwards, to a gracious time of her life.

One day, Idalynn said to Michael, "If the girls would like to return to me and finish their schooling in Lexington, I would absolutely love it! Dear Michael, would you mind sending them back to me?"

Michael did not want to linger on that subject, because the girls were not legally allowed to be in her care as long as they were minors; although, Lee was in college, and could certainly come and go as she pleased.

When Michael did discuss the possibility with Emily and Suzanne about returning to Lexington in the near future to be with their mother, neither girl wanted to leave their high school in Indiana. Emily was a senior, while Suzanne was a junior. By this time, they had established deep roots and lasting friendships. In all respects, Michael was relieved that he could put the onus on the girls rather than deny Idalynn their care.

Idalynn accepted the "no" answer reluctantly, and said she understood why the girls would not want to change schools at this point in the year. The promise that all would visit back and forth frequently was soothing for the moment.

Michael mentioned to Idalynn, that he would soon be retiring from the bench, and suggested that he, himself, might enjoy living in Lexington—of course, to be closer to the girls. He said he had always liked Lexington, and he could think of no better place to be, when the girls returned to her after high school.

Michael said, "It is my intention, and as far as I am concerned, my purpose in life, to always be, `just around the corner' from you. After all, we are family."

————————

Emily graduated top of her high school class, with plans of attending college at Indiana University in Bloomington. Nothing could please Idalynn more! Her daughter would be furthering her education.

One year later, Suzanne graduated from high school. Suzanne chose to follow her sister to Indiana University.

Lee chose to go to Antioch College in Yellowsprings, Ohio and was doing an internship at Columbia Broadcasting Station in Chicago. A smile came to Idalynn's face when she thought of how the family just didn't seem to get too far from Chicago—the city that possessed so much of her family's history.

Idalynn and Michael were very proud of their daughters. All three were enrolled in college. Michael had always stressed to his daughters, "Without an education, you are poor," so the girls always knew that their father had expected them to attend college.

It would soon be Homecoming weekend at the University in Lexington. Idalynn wanted very much to walk the campus that had been her path so many years ago. She invited Michael and their three daughters to enjoy the many festivities with her. Idalynn invited Michael to stay at their home. It seemed so strange now, after so many years of strife between them, that they were truly enjoying each other's company. There was a feeling of softness between them that had not existed for many years. Idalynn wondered if it was perhaps the ambience of just being back in her hometown in Mama's former home where they both had so many wonderful memories and where their romance that had started had created this atmosphere. Idalynn and the girls were looking forward to the wonderful weekend ahead.

At his home in Indiana, Michael was packing his clothes for his holiday in Lexington, when he fell ill. Feeling very strangely, Michael struggled to the telephone to call his neighbor next door, for assistance. His neighbor called an ambulance immediately and then rushed to Michael's apartment where he found Michael on the floor.

As he was riding in the ambulance, Michael couldn't help but remember the time, when he rode with his friend to the hospital in Chicago, many years ago. His thoughts wandered, and he smiled to himself, as he thought of all the past good times with Idalynn. He was especially proud of their girls. He silently thanked John Taylor, for his daughter, Suzanne.

Like his friend, John, Michael died before the ambulance reached the hospital. He had suffered a massive heart attack.

Answering the telephone, Idalynn said "Brooks' residence." Michael's neighbor introduced himself and hesitantly said, "Mrs Brooks, I am terribly distraught to inform you that Michael suffered a heart attack this morning and passed away on his way to the hospital in an ambulance. I was with Michael and he asked me to call you. I am so terribly sorry. Please tell me, what can I do to help you?"

Idalynn's head was reeling. The shock of hearing of Michael's death was more than she could bear. Weak and trembling, Idalynn placed a phone call to Emily and Suzanne at school in Bloomington and said, "Oh, children! A great tragedy has befallen all of us. Your father has died!" Lee was already enroute to Lexington and would be told upon her arrival at home.

It was difficult even to think of the coming weekend that would have been so enjoyable for all of them. Now they were mourning a great man who had loved all of them so much. Their "pillar" was gone. How would they ever be able to go on?

The girls cried for the loss of their father; Idalynn's tears flowed, for the loss of a wonderful man who had always been there standing behind her—in good times and in bad. Now he, too, was in her past. Throughout the silent night hours, Idalynn cried, grieved and thought of Michael.

———————

Emily took charge, and made all the arrangements for her father's funeral to be held in Indiana. At his funeral service, there were eleven former Treasury Agents from the Chicago area with whom he had worked side by side for many years.

One of the agents approached the family and said, "Michael Brooks was the best. He could have been exceedingly wealthy, but he was just too honest. Michael, most assuredly was an 'Untouchable'!"

There were so many like-comments about Michael. Whatever the various agents had to say about Michael to the family were only what they already knew. A very special man had departed this world.

Not even this small town where Michael had chosen to live and retire, were people aware that this very quiet man among their midst was such a giant to so many. No one was aware that he had been an 'Untouchable' or that Eliot Ness had slipped in and out of the town just to visit with Michael. Michael was that sort of private man.

———————

In death, Michael provided well for Idalynn and their three daughters. It was at this time that Idalynn was made aware, it had been Michael who was providing for their welfare, not her father. At one point, Charles Spencer had turned his back on all of them. Michael Brooks was the man who had loved them, unconditionally.

The home in Lexington was in her name, not the children's, as Michael had said it would be. Idalynn could not bear to think about all the years she had wasted, in not being a faithful wife and friend to dear Michael.

Enclosed with his will, was a personal note to Idalynn, addressed to "The Woman I Love." It read —

My Dearest Wife,

Idalynn, I call you 'wife,' as that is what you will always be to me, until the time of my death. From the moment that I saw you in your red ball gown, so many years ago, I knew you would be the only woman in my life, for the rest of my life!

Although we had some very sad interludes in our life together, try to look past those times and believe me when I say, I always held you in great esteem and always tried to do what was best for all of us, as a family. I am very sorry for any pain that my actions caused you during our marriage.

Know that I have left my estate to you and the girls, to be held in trust, and paid monthly to each of you. One more thing, Idalynn, as you will recall, I had a luncheon engagement with John Taylor on the day that he had his unfortunate accident. As you know, John and I had been friends for many years. We had a very long discussion that day about yours and his relationship. Although, I was disappointed, I could not in my heart fault John for how he felt about you. John had left the restaurant ahead of me, and as I came out, I saw the taxicab strike him, as he crossed the street. I ran to his side and held him in my arms. When the ambulance arrived, I was permitted to ride in the ambulance with him to the hospital.

While I was riding beside him in the ambulance, he told me about the expected baby. Before he died, he said to me, "Michael, if I don't make it through all this, I want my full estate to be given to the newly, expected baby, when he or she reaches the age of twenty-five. Maybe you could tell the baby, just a little something about me." He asked me to take care of all the details. I assured him that I would. I am pleased that John and I remained friends. When he departed from us, just a few minutes later, I felt honored to have held his hand. One of the medical men, in the ambulance, witnessed his wishes. I will still think of John as a very fine man. Never would I have betrayed him, by saying that I had proof that `our' baby was his."

Michael continued: Idalynn, promise me that you will tell Suzanne about John, if I have not done so, by the time you read this note. Do that for me. Idalynn, I have often wondered throughout the years, had I accepted your father's offer to work for him and stay in Lexington, would everything have been different between us?

Please note Idalynn, I leave my request to you to bury me in my town in Indiana. I have chosen to be buried here not only because I feel strong ties here, but in my mind, I will always be close by to all of you. I choose not to impose on you or your future life by requesting a burial in Lexington. However, should you ever choose to come in my direction, I have several burial locations for our family.

All I ask of you now, Idalynn, is your forgiveness for all the suffering that I did cause you. I have left a short note to our daughters.

Love,

Michael

To My Daughters,

Lee, you were my first-born and you gave purpose to my life. Emily, you are the one most like me. I have always been extremely proud of you. Suzanne, be assured that you were always a special addition to my life. I loved you all very much.

Daddy

———————————

Idalynn was heavy-hearted. Having read and reread Michael's letter to her, she realized now, much too late, that with Michael's death she had lost one of the dearest people in her life. She had been so blind to the fact that during the times when she thought him to be cruel and vengeful, he was trying to resolve the problems in the family. He always held out hope for a reconciliation of the family. And now, in death, he had taken care of all of them, with much affection.

After the funeral services and burial in Indiana, Idalynn made arrangements to reserve her own burial plot next to Michael. In the meantime, she would have Mama's grave moved to Indiana as well. It seemed the right thing to do since she had been so dependent on both of them in life. Michael would have liked this.

A few days later, the girls returned to school. Idalynn was alone at home. Memories surfaced as she walked through her gracious, but empty-feeling house, recalling her very young debutante days there.

She recalled the first time that Michael came to call. Michael had been so mesmerized with the beauty of the home. Of course, there was no possible way that he could have imagined the part this home would play in his future life.

Idalynn longed for the days when her father had been part of the family. She accepted the painful reality of her own responsibility for her parents not working out their difficulties, as ultimately belonging to her. She had to accept that blame. If truth were told, she had destroyed both of their lives.

Idalynn looked out of the window onto the grounds behind the house where at one time there had been stables for her father's racehorses. Now there was no evidence of such an area of where the horses had been trained and put through their paces. She saw only a cluster of small homes. Time had moved on; fate had led her full circle.

Idalynn only wished that her mother could have returned to her lovely home, and the lifestyle, that she had once possessed. It would have been Lulu Lee's dream to have been able to live out her life with the young man who came to Horse Cave selling his salts. In retrospect though, Idalynn also knew that Lulu Lee would not have changed anything if it would have meant not having her grandbabies to love.

Idalynn wondered to herself, *Where had all the years gone?* Reaching back in time, trying to solve the sad state of affairs, in which she had lived, and certainly caused, she wondered, *Why did I? If only. ...What if...?* But Idalynn knew, deservingly so, that the dark shadows from her life, would follow her forever.

As hard as she would try to step away from those shadows, Idalynn knew that she would have to bear the burden and certainly the responsibility of destruction to those she loved the most. Too late, the man that she now realized she had always loved, was gone.

Idalynn thought back to the time of her marriage. It was the love that she wanted to recall, not any of the pain. She thought about all the good things that Michael had done for her. She thought about how he had swept her off her feet—in Lexington. Those were the best times—when they were passionately in love—in Lexington.

Idalynn cried out to her mother, "Mama, I am so sorry. I promise you, I will never disappoint you again." To Michael, she vowed, "Thank you, Michael. You knew what was best for all of us. Please look down on me now, and know, I love you for all that you did for us. You always knew what was best."

Idalynn thought of her father, and remembered when she had rushed into her parent's bedroom after the dance to tell them all about meeting Michael. She thought to herself, "_Daddy, I am so like you. I am just so sorry that I hurt Mama,—as you did._"

It was dusk. There were many things that needed to be done. Knowing that sleep would elude her tonight, Idalynn decided to write the thank-you notes for Michael's funeral, on behalf of her family. This week, she and the girls would drive to Indiana, to care for Michael's possessions.

More importantly, she needed to sit down with the girls, and read their father's note to them. She needed to introduce to her family just who John Taylor was, and how he placed in the family. Suzanne needed to be told about her father, John. These were promises that had to be kept.

Idalynn's dreams were different now. In the months that followed, she involved herself with her daughters, whenever it was appropriate to do so. There were so many times when she was alone, when the tears and tender memories of her life with Michael would resurface.

Thinking back about her own life, Idalynn knew that, for a passage of time, she had lived a privileged life. Now, it was necessary for her conquer the sadness encompassing her, and accept a new life that was destined to her. She simply had to adjust to a new life alone. Only she was responsible for her own destiny; and she knew she could not just wait for it to come to her. She had to face the future.

How long had it been since she had laughed? Idalynn couldn't remember. But by chance one evening when she was reading the newspaper, her eyes drifted to a story about the need for daycare in the Lexington area for homeless mothers who were raising their children alone. Idalynn felt as though she had experienced an awakening. Where would she or her children have ended up had it not been for someone standing along side of her?

Idalynn felt as though she had found a purpose in her life. She knew what she wanted to do. Ironically, while she had basically turned the care of her own children over to someone else, now it was she who wanted to assist others in the care of their children.

Idalynn's own passion of conviction in these matters pushed her in the direction of the possibilities of turning Mulberry into a special home for very special children, and every child was special. After all, Idalynn did know how it felt to be homeless.

Wanting to be like Mama who had taken young girls into her home so that she could prepare them for a decent future life, Idalynn wanted to help the innocent young babies that needed someone to care for them—as her own mother had given her life to care for her grandbabies. Idalynn's brightest hours were about to begin….

Idalynn proceeded at once to call upon her social friends—even some who had been her own students in kindergarten—to help her bring this dream to reality. A proposal to the community needed to be drawn to convince the people of the worthiness of such a project. After filing proper paper work for a license, staff would need to be hired

Within a short few weeks, many people were responding to Idalynn's dream of Mulberry turning into a special place for little boys and girls to receive special attention and most importantly, feel loved. Idalynn could not express her gratitude enough.

In months to follow, there was a dramatic expansion to Mulberry. Idalynn was personally involved in the decor of every room. She gave endlessly with her time and energy. Each room was designed around a special nursery tale, and offered a sense of adventure for any child who entered.

Soon the imposing doors of Mulberry opened to the children. Idalynn stood at the entrance, smiling and welcoming each little visitor, directing them to their special room. It was so heartwarming to watch the children gleefully run to their fairy tale rooms, just as fast as their little legs would carry them.

Idalynn enjoyed watching the children at play in her home. She was reminded of the time in her life when she had been the teacher to so many little ones. Tears welled in her eyes when one expressionless child asked Idalynn, "Are you my mama?"

At last, Idalynn felt that her life had a purpose and a spirited meaning to it. More importantly, a wiser, stronger and loving woman had emerged. With certainty, Idalynn finally knew that she was where she was suppose to be. She was committed to the children.

Over the years, Lexington honored her for sharing her life and home. The city was eternally grateful to this remarkable woman whose portrait hung in the vestibule of Mulberry. As people entered Mulberry they would gaze at this portrait of the elegant-looking woman who possessed an aura that personified tenderness and love. The questions asked were, "Who is she? I wonder what kind of life she had lived? I wonder if she was some sort of grand dame? Maybe someday someone will write a book about her!"

Idalynn, in turn, was grateful to the people of Lexington for assisting her with her dreams. She felt needed in Lexington. Never did she feel the need for any acknowledgment from anyone. The happy sounds of the children were comforting to her and were what she loved the most. These were truly the best of times!

Then one day, Idalynn Brooks grew weary and collapsed.

The plane touched down at the Lexington Airport. Upon deplaning, Suzanne was met by her sister, Emily. They drove directly to Mulberry, where their mother resided upstairs. Rushing past the various children's nursery rooms and up the grand staircase to her mother's bedroom, Suzanne found a doctor attending her. Lee was standing next to her mother's bedside.

Upon Suzanne entering the room, Idalynn stretched out her arms to her and said, "Oh, Suzanne, how wonderful to see you! Dr. Edmonds, this is my youngest daughter, Suzanne. Suzanne, meet Dr. Marshall Edmonds. I knew his father, well."

Although Idalynn and Dr. Edmonds had already enjoyed a discussion regarding her engagement to his father many years ago, Idalynn did not allude to this to Suzanne.

Dr. Edmonds put forth his hand and said, "Hello, Suzanne. I understand that we were once, almost, a family! That might have been fun!" With her thoughts completely on her mother, Suzanne did not question his remark, but let it slip past.

When Idalynn dozed off to sleep, Dr. Edmonds asked the three daughters to step out with him into the hall, while a nurse attended to their mother. In doing so, he advised the girls that their mother was very ill, and that more than likely, her very weakened heart would give out within a short period of time. He assured the girls, that he would continue to stay with their mother through the night, and make her as comfortable as possible.

The three sisters assured the doctor that they had no intentions of leaving their mother's side.

The girls thought back to the story that their grandmother had so often told them of their mother's birth when she weighed only a pound and a half. At the time, the doctor in attendance of the birth had said, "This little girl does have a weak heart but with her spirit and determination that she is already showing us, I believe that she will make it!" Now it appeared that her spirit and determination were leaving her, and with that her heart would give up as well. By morning, Idalynn had suffered a setback, with pneumonia settling in her lungs.

The first thing that Idalynn said to her girls that morning was, "Your father was here just a little while ago. We had such a nice talk. We are so proud of our daughters." There was a silence in the room as the girls looked among each other.

Idalynn continued, "You know girls, my mama would be so pleased to know that we have all remained, so close. Know that it was wonderful, for all of us to have remained together, as a family. Please remember, Mama, your Daddy and I loved you all so very much."

Later that day, Idalynn passed away with her three daughters, and Dr. Edmonds, at her bedside. The three sisters were bereft with grief, and struggled to contain themselves. They knew that putting together a funeral service for their mother would be a very difficult thing to do.

It was only fitting that Mulberry continued functioning during these very stressful times. Idalynn would have wanted nothing less. Unbeknownst to the children playing downstairs, a godmother of sorts to them had passed from this earth.

Idalynn was buried in the Indiana Cemetery next to her mother, Lulu Lee, with Michael buried on the other side of her. Surely, Michael's smile that Idalynn had once said, "was like a magnificent sunset," was smiling on her once again.

The only family member not buried there was Charles. The sisters could only hope that perhaps Charles and Lulu Lee had found one another again. And maybe, just maybe, he has already said to her, "I do beg your forgiveness," as he had once said to her so very long ago when he had first met her. That was the day she had dropped her parcels, when his car had backfired.

Over time, a wonderful friendship developed between Lee and Dr. Marshall Edmonds, and shortly thereafter, a lovely romance began. Within one year, Lee, feeling such a strong bond to her grandparents' and mother's home, planned her wedding to Marshall to take place in front of the marble fireplace, where Idalynn and Michael had married before. Since Marshall had his practice established in Lexington, a city that Lee had already drawn claim to, the young couple was delighted to remain there. Idalynn could not have planned it better.

Emily married a scientist from Lawrenceburg, Indiana. They had met during their high school days, while Emily lived with her father. How nice that Lawrenceburg was just across the river from Kentucky.

Suzanne returned to Kansas City to her career in the skies. In time, she met and married a pilot for Trans World Airlines. Knowing Suzanne's inherent ties to the state of Kentucky, her husband suggested that they move to Lexington to live where he could fly out of the Blue Grass Airport to commute to his flights. Suzanne smiled and thought to herself, "In my heart, I couldn't have planned it better. Why would anyone want to leave Kentucky?" (Great Grandfather Taylor would have been very proud.)

Epilogue

As fate would play out, in later years, the Spencer mansion, or "Mulberry," was razed to make room for the Adolph Rupp Arena. For a short period of time, Mulberry, was relocated to another part of town. With generations to come, the name *Mulberry* eventually lost its place in history. Mulberry had ended.

Angeline Taylor had always loved her home, Mulberry, in Horse Cave, and had implored her daughters and sons to return there. While Lulu Lee always felt a strong need to return to Horse Cave, it was necessary to accept Lexington's Mulberry, as her home.

In turn, Mulberry, in Lexington, always had a profound hold on Idalynn, never allowing her to disconnect herself from her Kentucky path to yesterday. The three daughters always discussed among themselves of their own similar feelings of a surreal-like-draw that they too always felt to Kentucky.

When the three sisters asked the doctor to explain to them how it was possible that their mother could have ever been diagnosed as a sociopath with psychosis, he had two answers for them.

"A person could be diagnosed as such, as a result of emotional deprivation from those whom a person loves; consequently, causing that person to lose contact with reality.

From what you all have told me, all the signs seemed to show that your mother was summarily affected while growing up. Your mother had a self-destructive behavior as a young girl. She refused to be corralled. She refused to assume any responsibilities.

Perhaps, as a result of having been attended by servants, who bestowed much attention upon her during her young life, was a contributing factor. She was never able or perhaps, never allowed, to make her own decisions; and when she finally did, the results were disastrous. However, from her past medical history, she was diagnosed as having had a mental disorder. You know, it was not until 1941 when a Psychiatric Diagnostic Statistical Manual of Mental Disorders was published. This publication was so that all doctors would be on the same page with their diagnosis, rather than just drawing their own conclusions. Previously, many patients, perhaps even your mother, could have been misdiagnosed prior to this new knowledge. There may well have been a misdiagnosis in this case. Today, we speak of these types of patients as having a borderline personality."

Idalynn's legacy was now immortalized. The girls were in agreement that perhaps one of her greatest faults in life was that of loving Lexington too much. And too, while some of her life had been lived as not the best mother, she did love her children and tried to care for them in the best way that she knew how. No one would dispute the fact that Idalynn, at times, was unyielding to others, accepting no blame, but she always possessed the determination to assure we children, that we were special.

The three sisters were in complete acceptance of the fact, that although Mama had been the caretaker, their mother had contributed much to their lives in the sense of self esteem. Looking back, that was perhaps the greatest thing that she did for them. With her death, the girls possessed a sense of gratitude toward their mother and realized it was easier to try to forget any of her faults, and remember only her virtues. What was important now was to draw strength from the past.

To this day, the three sisters know that they were fortunate to have known Mama, Mother and Daddy. They wondered had they been given the opportunity, would they have known and loved their grandfather, Daddy Spencer as well? While Daddy Spencer or "Mr. Charlie," as he was known by so many in Lexington, was a highly influential man, and made life better for so many, he never realized the negative consequences of his own actions during his lifetime, of his greatest legacy – his three grandchildren or more importantly, the love of his three grandchildren.

Lee, Emily and Suzanne have never chosen to relive their past; after all, they had lived it once. Looking back, one would surmise that with this journey, life had come full circle. Life began and ended in Kentucky for the Taylor and Spencer families; while the Edmonds family that had at one time played an important part in Idalynn's life, was now, once again, connected to the Spencer family through the marriage of Marshall and Lee. Marshall knows that his father, Roger would have approved.

Lee, Emily and Suzanne have never severed the close bonds that kept them together during their traumatic childhoods. In their hearts, they will hold forever the memories of their lives together and will always be proud of their lives and heritage. Lulu Lee, Idalynn and Michael would be proud.